THE INNER KNIGHT

TRAIN AND COMPETE LIKE A CHAMPION

BILLY KETCH ALLEN

MOONGLASS
BOOKS

Copyright © 2022 Billy Ketch Allen
All rights reserved.

This is a work of fiction. Names, characters, places, and incidents either are the product of the author's imagination or are used fictitiously. Any resemblance to actual persons, living or dead, events, or locales is entirely coincidental.

Published by Moonglass Books
First Edition 2022

ISBN 978-0-9886365-2-1

Thank you for supporting the author's work.

Also by Billy Ketch Allen

Fiction

Good Blood

Dark Blood

Requiem For House Octavian

Nonfiction

Coach Your Brains Out

(with John Mayer)

The Letter

News has reached me that you are preparing for your first tournament. I remember the excitement of my early years and only wish I'd aligned that passion with better training. It is for this reason that I write to you—to offer encouragement and to share the lessons I've learned.

The path of a competitor is a difficult one, full of pain and sacrifice. Yet I would not trade it for any other. I have dedicated my life to the pursuit of excellence and, through hard work, have found fulfillment greater than any treasure. But I did not walk this path alone.

At a time when I needed it most, I met a teacher. I was angry and lost, and his methods were like a lantern in the night. He taught me how to practice the training and the trusting mindsets. He taught me to be aware of my emotions and to act independently of my feelings. He taught me to stay within my three-foot world and to harness the power of the present moment. And he taught me the importance of living out my values, on the tournament field and beyond. It is because of his lessons that I have achieved all I have and learned the true meaning of honor.

I have torn up the pages that follow again and again, unsure of how to present what I've learned. For if you share any of my stubbornness, you will not heed a list of rules. So, I will follow my teacher's example. He taught me the power of stories, how they stay with us, their lessons burrowing a home in our hearts.

This is my story.

—Meridian Kay

Morning Lessons

As the daughter of a Scottish noble family, it was expected I spend my days practicing the meaningless skills of a lady. That is why I found myself, one cloudless summer morning, jumping out the upper window of our estate.

I hit the ground with a heavy thud and spilled onto my side. Wincing, I climbed to my feet and brushed dirt from my dress. Mother wouldn't be happy. But I'd had enough of sewing lessons. It was too nice a day to be trapped indoors.

I hurried across the courtyard to the stable. Snowfoot looked up from his stall. The horse nodded excitedly as I approached.

"Hey, boy." I patted his reddish-brown coat. "Care for a ride?"

Snowfoot stomped, showing off the signature white markings above each hoof. I'd picked him out when I was twelve years old and he was just a foal. The farmer selling him had thought me crazy, saying everyone knows a horse with four white feet is unlucky. But I didn't care. From the moment I saw him, I knew Snowfoot was the horse for me.

I opened the gate and led him out of his stall. There was no time to saddle him. My dress ripped as I climbed onto his back. Snowfoot snorted and shook his head. "I don't need to hear it from you, too," I said.

Snowfoot trotted across the stable. I pulled his black mane, stopping him at the door to check for any sign of my mother. The courtyard was quiet.

"Let's go," I whispered, tapping Snowfoot's sides with my slippered feet. I ducked my head as he galloped across the courtyard, afraid I'd hear my name shouted from behind me. But a moment later, we were through the gates. I smiled as the warm wind blew my hair back, and I let go of Snowfoot's mane. He didn't need direction. He rode straight across the field to the practice grounds.

Growing up, I had no interest in the games of other girls, and the dolls my parents bought me remained on their shelves. Instead, I played alone in the courtyard, swinging sticks at imaginary enemies, defeating battalions of English soldiers or dueling the legendary Grey Knight. For ever since I could remember, I'd had but one dream: to become a champion knight.

I attended my first tournament at age six and immediately fell in love with jousting. My father was a local Scottish champion and, having no son, indulged my interest. He taught me to ride and to joust, how the proper positioning of the lance could make up for my lack of strength, how a connection with one's horse was often overlooked by other knights, and how, when charging toward an opponent of equal skill, the winner would be the one who better mastered his fear.

My father believed my training harmless, that I would eventually give up wanting to be a knight and settle on an interest befitting a lady. But by the age of seventeen, my passion for jousting had only grown. He may have let me continue my foolish dream had my mother not intervened. Women did not engage in such sport; they did not come home bruised and dirty. My mother ruled it long past time I outgrew my fantasy and accepted who I was. She forbade me from jousting and filled my day with more appropriate tasks. If she had her way, the closest I would come to a tournament would be watching from the pavilion, awarding a token to an honorable knight—a scarf I'd sewn myself.

I slowed Snowfoot as we reached the practice grounds. The simple dirt field was my favorite place in the world. As a young girl, I'd spent countless hours there, jousting with blunted lances, or honing my aim catching rings on the practice post until the last light of day slipped behind the hills and darkness finally called me home.

We waited at the edge of the practice grounds and watched my father train. William Kay was thin for a knight and little taller than me—my mother's height was one gift I was thankful for. But in his practice armor, sitting atop his brown destrier, Bridgewater, my father seemed as mighty as the Grey Knight himself.

The boy on the smaller grey horse was Roland, my cousin of thirteen. He served as a page, tending to the horses, for which he had a true talent. After a few years serving as a page under my father, Roland would advance to a squire and then, if he proved himself worthy, he would be knighted. Such was the path for a noble boy.

"Again, Roland," my father called. "And keep your lance steady this time. I'll not suffer a blow to Bridgewater."

My father and Roland faced each other from opposite ends of the dirt track, raising long wooden lances. "Yah!" my father's voice boomed. The two horses cantered, picking up speed. A joust only lasts a few seconds. Most spectators shift their eyes from one rider to the next, caught up in the tension of the coming collision. But I kept my eyes on Roland as he rode along the right side of the rope barrier, spotting the small inefficiencies in his movements: the wide elbow, causing the lance to wobble; bending low in the saddle, leaving him unable to attack with power; his lance angled too low for an effective strike. In the seconds it took Roland's horse to reach speed, my mind had weighed his weaknesses and found the most effective attack.

So had my father. Roland's lance struck weakly at my father's waist, while my father's covered coronel rammed into Roland's breastplate. Roland flew off his horse and crashed to the ground. The grey reared up with a screech and galloped away.

"Unhorsed again, Roland?" I called. "Your lance is too low."

Roland tore off his helmet and glared at me. "Shouldn't you be inside brushing your hair?"

My father brought Bridgewater around. He raised his visor to me, part in salute, part in suspicion. "What are you doing here, Meridian? If your mother finds out..."

"She gave me a break," I said. "Since I've been working so hard."

Roland scoffed. "Drinking tea and sewing is exhausting work."

"That's enough, Roland," my father said. "And Meridian is right. If you worry about your opponent's lance, you sacrifice your own attack. A knight cannot be afraid to take a blow."

"I'm not afraid," Roland said.

"Aye, lad. You just need more practice getting hit."

"And keeping your lance higher," I added.

Roland's face reddened. "Like you could do better."

"Care to find out?" I rode Snowfoot across the track to the armory and drew a practice lance from the rack. The smooth wood felt at home in my hands.

"This is ridiculous," Roland said. "Girls can't joust."

"What's the matter, Roland? Afraid of getting hit?"

"There'll be no jousting," my father said. "I'll not hear the end of this if one of you breaks an arm. You can settle this on the practice rings."

Roland frowned, unable to refuse the challenge in front of my father. "Fine," he said. "Seven passes. And after I beat you, you stay away from the practice grounds and leave jousting to the men."

I smiled. "Perhaps you should retrieve your mount first, oh noble knight."

Roland huffed and stormed into the field after his horse.

"You shouldn't tease your cousin, Meridian," my father said. He removed his helmet and wiped his forehead. "He's a good lad, and he's been a help to our family."

"I'm sorry. But it's not fair that he gets to train and I don't. After you, I'm the best jouster within a two-day ride."

"If only I had taught you humility as well as courage." My father smirked.

"Please, Father, take me to York with you. I know women can't be knights, but surely I could act as your squire. Tending to Bridgewater and polishing your armor isn't complicated work. And I'd give anything to see the Tournament of Champions."

Since it had been announced, the King of England's Tournament of Champions had been all I could think about. It was the first event of its kind, inviting the top knights from all over Europe. If my father placed high, it would make a name for our family. And if he won, the prize purse would put an end to our debts. I fantasized about standing beside my father on the tournament field, the crowd chanting "Sir Kay."

"Treaty or no treaty, England is a dangerous place, Meridian," my father said. "And besides, I'm not in the tournament yet."

"You're one of the best knights in Scotland! The king has to invite you!"

"My daughter may not be the best judge, I'm afraid."

"It's true. You'd have even beaten the Grey Knight."

My father chuckled. "Now I know you can't be trusted." His smile faded, and he stared into the distance. "I saw him once, you know."

"What!" I exclaimed. I thought my father had told me every jousting story he knew. How had he never mentioned meeting the legendary English champion, the knight every other jouster was measured against?

"It wasn't at a tournament," he said, as if reading my thoughts. "I was a young soldier when we marched to reclaim Berwick. We had the English outnumbered and surrounded on Halidon Hill. Our men were already cheering our victory when he emerged from the English ranks. It was as if a legend had jumped from the pages of a book. He was as big as two men and wore grey armor with an eagle emblem atop his helm. The Grey Knight cut through our ranks with a lance as long as a tree. There was no more cheering that day." My father shuddered as if still haunted by the memory.

"What happened to him?" I asked.

"He died in battle, most likely. Though the king hid it to perpetuate the legend. Every man serves, even in death."

"Every man," I muttered to myself. "I'm not afraid to fight, father. If I only had the chance."

"I know, Meridian. But this world has its laws, and we must each follow the path before us."

My hands tightened on Snowfoot's mane. "What if I don't like my path?"

"Then you'll spend your life fighting through brambles." He gave me a sympathetic smile.

Across the track, Roland had recovered his horse and was waiting at the practice post. "Now," my father said, "go show Roland how it's done."

I leaned over Snowfoot, falling into the rhythm of his gait. My eyes locked on my target—the medallion-sized metal ring hanging from the arm of the post. I struck out in a clean thrust and caught the ring on the tip of my lance. I smiled as I pulled Snowfoot to a stop and held the ring high. "Four for four."

Roland grunted and turned his horse around to start his next pass. He had only caught one ring. I took a deep breath and petted Snowfoot's neck. How I'd missed this.

Roland finished his next pass with a curse, having missed the ring completely. My confidence was high as I started my next pass. I was already thinking of my inevitable victory as I began my thrust, and the ring slipped from the end of my lance.

"I guess you're not perfect after all," Roland said.

I felt my face flush but held my tongue. My father was watching. I thought through my pass, searching for what I'd done wrong. Had I flared my elbow? Was I overreaching? I felt my father's eyes on me, his disappointment like a crushing weight. Whatever rhythm I'd had was gone. I missed catching the ring on the next two passes, each time worse than the last. I pulled Snowfoot to a stop and hurled my lance onto the ground.

"Roland," my father said. "Practice isn't over. Go fetch our lances."

"Yes, sir," Roland said, and rode back to the armory.

"I still beat him," I said. I'd caught four rings to Roland's two, but the victory felt hollow.

"Roland wasn't your opponent," my father said. "A knight must be as strong mentally as physically. You have the skill, Meridian, but you lose focus. When you're working with your mother, you're thinking about jousting. When you're jousting, you're worried about what others think. You'll never reach your full potential until you learn to keep your head and your feet in the same place."

I wanted to ask him how I was supposed to improve when I wasn't allowed to practice, but a shrill call stopped me cold. "Meridian!"

My handmaid's stocky figure trudged through the field toward the practice grounds.

"Young lady!" Eby huffed, her shoe catching in the soft dirt. "You can't go running off in the middle of your lessons. And look at you! Your dress is filthy!"

I winced, unable to meet my father's eyes.

"You lied to me," he said.

"I only meant to watch, really."

The look of disappointment on my father's face stung worse than any blow. "Go," he said. "You must honor your mother." He put his helmet on and grabbed Bridgewater's reins. "And remember what I said. When you're jousting, joust. When you're working, work."

I watched him ride across the practice grounds, wishing with all my heart I could go with him.

Eby reached me, panting. "We must return at once. Your mother is furious."

"I don't care," I said, turning Snowfoot back toward our estate. "She's already taken jousting from me. What more can she do?"

Despite being out of breath, Eby gave me an earful as she kept pace with Snowfoot. Halfway across the field, I glanced back to the practice grounds where my father and Roland continued to train, their lances raised as if in salute to the heavens. The unfairness of the image sent a stab of pain through me. Any hope I'd had of attending the Tournament of Champions slipped away. My father was right. The course of our lives is set from birth, and no matter how much I wanted it, my path had nothing to do with jousting.

A Messenger Arrives

"You still insist on rolling around in the dirt with your father and Roland," Eby shook her head; the strings of her coif slapped side to side. "It's time you grew up and saw the wisdom in your mother's plans."

"Jonathan Alison, you mean."

"There are harder things in this world than marrying a rich lord."

"I don't mind hard things, Eby. It's boring ones I can't stand."

We reached the edge of the field when a rider appeared on the road. My heart dropped at the sight of the satchel slung across his saddle. A messenger.

"I'll meet you inside, Eby," I said, and spurred Snowfoot into a run.

"Meridian!" Eby called after me, but her cries died in the wind.

I pulled Snowfoot to a stop and intercepted the rider before our gates. He wore a red surcoat with gold trim—an extravagant garment for a messenger. It was clear what my mother expected to gain from a union with the Alisons.

"Morning, good sir," I said, blocking his path. "You carry a message?"

"A letter for Lord William Kay," he said.

"Entrust it to me, and I'll see that my father gets it."

"Thank you, but I have orders to deliver the letter to Lord Kay himself."

"And nothing would give me greater pleasure than escorting you to his door. But I fear my father has fallen ill."

"Sick you say?"

"He remains bedridden, covered in boils and burning with fever."

The messenger's face tightened as he squinted past me to our manor house.

"But orders are orders," I said. "Come, I'll show you to his chambers. Though you'll have to forgive the smell."

"Hold now." The messenger reached into his satchel. "I see no harm in trusting the letter to a lady of the house. You will take it to him directly?"

I bowed. "On my word as a lady."

"Very well." He held out the letter. "I thank you, Lady Kay, and pray for your father's recovery."

"As do we all." I took the letter and coughed into my hand. The messenger spun his horse and, without a second glance, shot down the road in a cloud of dust. I smiled and then set off for the stable to destroy the letter.

Over the past year, my mother had redoubled her efforts to arrange a suitable marriage for me, negotiating in my father's name. My family's status had fallen of late, so I was not Lord Alison's first choice for his son. Unfortunately, my mother's skill with a pen rivaled my father's with a lance, and a union with Jonathan Alison had become very much a reality.

I pulled Snowfoot into his stall and had hardly dismounted when my name rang through the stable. "Meridian!"

I jumped at my mother's voice. Darting to the wall, I stuffed Lord Alison's letter between two hay bales.

"There you are," my mother snapped. She strode through the stable, holding up her dress to avoid the dirt. Her steely eyes fixed upon me, and I thought for a moment she'd caught me hiding the letter.

"You abandoned your lessons once again," she said.

"I'm sorry, Mother. I wanted to watch Father train. I only meant to be gone a few minutes." I ran my hand through Snowfoot's mane, avoiding her stern glare.

"You are a high-born lady. What proposals would we get if noble lords discovered you spent your days playing in the dirt?"

"If a man is intimidated by that, then I have no interest in him."

"Enough, Meridian! I won't suffer your childish disobedience any longer. You know the hardships our family suffers. Our only hope of repaying our debts and keeping our lands is through marriage. Fortunately, our only daughter is in possession of beauty, if not obedience. And we must each work with what we are given."

"You'd really sell me off to the Alisons to pay the rent?"

My mother's face hardened. "I will do whatever is necessary to save this family."

"Our debts will be repaid as soon as Father wins the Tournament of Champions."

My mother scoffed. "Your father's dreams are as foolish as your own, Meridian. This Tournament of Champions is a farce. It's designed to show England's superiority. No Scot can win."

"You're wrong. Father will go to York, and he'll defeat the English and bring honor to our family name."

My mother's hands tightened on her dress. "Tournaments and pageants don't bring honor. Putting your family's needs before your pride does."

"At least he's trying to pay our debts, not selling off his daughter like some prized cow!"

"That's enough!" My mother stood up straight. "Since you refuse to obey, you leave me no choice. We will sell this horse of yours on the morrow."

"What! Snowfoot? You can't!"

"I can, and I will. It's for your own good, Meridian. Someday you'll understand."

My legs wobbled as if I'd been struck. I fell back against Snowfoot's stall and clung to his neck. His coarse hair pressed against my cheek. Snowfoot was all I had left. I wouldn't let her take him from me.

Before I could say anything, shouts erupted outside. Frantic yelling filled the courtyard. A field worker rushed past the stable door. My mother called to him, demanding to know what was going on.

"Lady Kay." He looked at us, his face pale as bone. "You must come quick. There's been an accident on the practice grounds!"

Shattered Lance

Servants carried my father to my parents' chambers. I called to him, hoping to hear his voice telling me not to worry, that everything was all right. But he didn't answer. He lay still, his practice armor marred with dirt and blood.

I wandered outside, trying to get the image of my father's body out of my head. Roland paced the courtyard, still wearing his breastplate. He flinched when he saw me. "How is he?" he asked, voice cracking.

"I don't know," I said. "Mother won't let me see him. No one will tell me anything. Roland, what happened?"

"We were jousting. I struck him high, just above the breastplate, a lucky shot for I . . . I'd never landed a solid blow before." Roland looked down. "Oh, Lord."

"What?" I seized Roland by the shoulders as if to rattle the story from him. "Roland, what happened?"

"My lance shattered," he said. "A piece must have struck Uncle William under the helmet. I heard an awful noise and turned back to see him fall beneath Bridgewater."

I let go of Roland and stepped back.

"He wasn't moving, and the blood..." Roland was whimpering now, his face streaked with dirty tears. "Tell me it's not true, Mer. Tell me I didn't kill him."

"Of course not! Don't say such rubbish. Father took a fall, that is all."

I turned, pushing Roland's words from my head. But doubt seized me, tightening around my belly, squeezing my chest. I wheezed, unable to breathe. I raced back inside, taking the stairs in leaps. He was my father; they had to let me see him. I would attend to him, get him back on his feet. The Tournament of Champions was still months away. We had time...

I reached the second-floor landing and stopped. Servants crowding the hall fell silent at the sight of me. They looked at the floor. I wanted to shout at them to leave. There was nothing to worry about—my father would be fine. Instead, I tottered through the hall with my head down. Dark spots stained the stone floor. My father's blood.

The door to my parents' chambers opened. My mother stumbled out, clutching her stomach.

"Mother?" For a moment I thought she'd been stabbed. Her eyes settled on mine, and I knew.

"No," I stammered. "No, no, no..."

My mother swallowed and pulled herself up. "Meridian—"

"No, it's not true."

She reached a hand toward me and then stopped as if the effort were too great. "Your father is dead."

"No. You're wrong."

Her voice was flat, lifeless. "Come pay your respects."

I stepped back, recoiling from the door. "No, he has to be all right. The tournament..."

"There is no tournament!" she snapped. Her jaw tightened, and she began to shake. "There is no treasure to save us. Your father is dead!"

"No!" I yelled, backing away. "I'm done listening to you. I won't let you sell Snowfoot. I won't let you sell me!"

"Meridian! Get back here this minute!"

My mother's voice chased me down the stairs, but I kept running. Away from her, and away from what lay inside that room. I reached my quarters, slammed the door and crumbled to the floor. I squeezed my eyes shut, trying to make it all go away. That morning my father had been larger than life, riding Bridgewater like a hero from a fable, and now . . .

I don't know how long I lay on the floor, but when I finally got control of myself, my mind was made up. The debt collectors could seize our lands and tear the estate to the ground for all I cared. This wasn't my home anymore. I was done being Lady Kay.

I crossed the room to my dresser and emptied the contents onto the floor. I put on a shirt and britches, boots, and a travel cloak. Then I packed extra clothes into a sack. I made my way downstairs to the kitchen and filled the rest of the sack with what provisions I could find. I didn't know where I'd go; all I knew was that I couldn't stay there.

I snuck across the courtyard to the stable and threw my arms around Snowfoot. He snorted and sniffed my hair. His breath was heavy and warm.

"It's just you and me now, boy." Somewhere in the horse's deep black eyes, I saw he understood.

I lifted a saddle onto his back and ran the girth under his belly. I flung my travel sack over my shoulder and was about to leave when I remembered the letter. In a flash of anger, I stormed to the hay bales and pulled the letter from its hiding place. I tore off the ribbon and was about to rip the letter to pieces when I noticed the seal. My finger ran over the swirling symbol stamped in red wax. The letter was not from Lord Alison.

I broke the seal and unrolled the parchment. I could not read well, but I knew enough to understand what I was holding. In my hands was a letter from the King of England, inviting my father to the Tournament of Champions.

My head spun. I fell against the hay bales. Why had I not taken the letter directly to my father? If I'd done as I was told, he would have lived to see his dream come true.

I steadied myself and looked again at the name written in curved scrawl across the top of the letter. "Sir William Kay," I whispered.

I carefully rolled the invitation and retied the ribbon. Then I placed the letter in my pocket. Snowfoot stomped a white foot, watching me.

"Come on, boy," I said. "It's not over." I climbed into the saddle, and we fled through the open gates and across the field.

Clouds gathered overhead, blotting out the once blue sky. We reached the practice grounds, and I dismounted. I left Snowfoot and entered the armory shed. My father had fallen in his practice armor, but his tournament armor was still there. I unlocked the oak chest and looked at the polished armor that had cost a fortune. My father had shined in that armor. In Edinburgh, he'd dueled the best knights in Scotland. He'd been a hero that day. He'd made a name for himself, for our family.

I lifted the helmet and studied the narrow eye-slits. With the visor down, the face would be completely hidden. No one would know the knight inside. In this armor, I could become someone else.

I loaded my father's armor into its travel packs and slung them over the back of the saddle. Snowfoot grunted under the weight and staggered forward. "Easy, boy." I walked him to the rack and drew a short practice lance. I strapped the lance to the side of his saddle and climbed on. Snowfoot snorted but held steady.

I took one last look at the practice grounds: the dirt spotted with hoofprints, the rope barrier that hung from its poles, the practice post that stood like a cross over the ground where my father had fallen. These grounds had been special to me once. A place where I felt strong and free. Where I could escape life as a noble lady and be anything I wanted. Even a knight.

The sun had set by the time we reached the main road. I didn't slow for fear I'd lose my courage. I gripped the reins and pressed my head against Snowfoot. We rode south, into the dark. We rode to England.

Roads and Apples

The road south stretched endlessly. I kept my distance from other travelers as I crossed into England. Tension from years of fighting don't disappear with the signing of a treaty. I ran out of provisions after two days, and the hunger crept from my gut to my head and limbs until my whole body groaned for food. But weak as I was, I kept riding. Pride would not allow me to turn back.

The nights were cold, and I slept on the ground in a bed of extra clothes. I couldn't help but think how different the journey would have been if my father were with me, sharing stories of tournaments and of war with the English. I fell asleep shivering, convinced he was watching over me.

One afternoon I was walking beside Snowfoot, to ease his burden and to relieve the soreness of a long day spent in the saddle, when I came upon five men. The men stood on the side of the road beside their horses. Upon seeing me, their conversation stopped. A man with curly blond hair that matched his floor-length golden coat stepped into the road and blocked my path.

"Tell me," he said, looking me over. "Why's a pretty lass like you traveling all by herself?"

"That's no concern of yours," I said.

"A Scot, too?" He looked at his companions, and his smile widened. "These roads are dangerous, girl. You'd do well to have some protection."

"I can handle myself."

He looked at Snowfoot and snickered. "Four white feet is bad luck, you know. What's the saying, boys? 'One white foot, keep him to the end. Two white feet, sell him to a friend. Three white feet, send him far away...'"

"Four white feet, keep him not a day," called a large, bearded man with cruel eyes.

"Is that why you're here alone? Happened upon some bad luck?"

"I'm not alone," I said, moving closer to Snowfoot. "I'm meeting my father. He is expecting me."

"That's his armor you're carrying, then?" the blond-haired man smiled. "I'm surprised he'd trust such an expensive suit with a little girl."

"She's not so little," called one of his companions. "Tall as a man. And she looks ready to bite."

The men laughed.

My hands balled into fists at my side. "Step aside," I demanded.

"Of course," the man said with a bow, his golden locks falling from his shoulders. "Safe travels."

My hands shook as I climbed into the saddle. "Yah," I said, before I'd even seized the reins. Snowfoot broke into a run. Behind me, the men stood in the road, watching me go.

I put an hour of hard riding in before my nerves finally settled. It was then that the reality of my situation struck me. I was alone in a strange country with no food or money and nothing for protection but a dulled training lance. The Tournament of Champions didn't start for months. And even if I survived that long, how was I going to fool a city of people into thinking I was Sir William Kay? The farther I rode from home, the more absurd it all seemed.

The road cut through a thick forest whose canopy blocked the sun. It was in these shadows that I heard the hoofbeats. Five riders were coming up the road behind me. The lead rider wore a golden coat.

"Ride." I slapped Snowfoot's reins. "Ride!"

Snowfoot tore down the road. I gritted my teeth and ducked under the whipping wind as we fled through the forest. But the hoofbeats grew louder. Snowfoot was slowing, his breath coming in heavy gasps. I'd pushed him too long. I pictured the men's greedy faces and knew I couldn't let them catch me.

Around the next sharp bend, I turned off the road. The forest was dense, but Snowfoot plunged through, jumping over logs and crashing through thick brambles. When we'd gone far enough, I yanked the reins. Snowfoot skidded to a stop. I jumped off and pulled him behind a tree, holding his head to keep him still. His breath was ragged and hot.

"Quiet now," I pleaded, pressing my face against his. "Shhh."

The hoofbeats sounded like thunder. I stopped breathing, fearing I hadn't pulled far enough off the road. They would see us for sure. But the five men rode past, disappearing around the next bend.

I stood frozen, even after their hoofbeats had faded away, afraid to return to the road. I was a fool to run away, a fool to think I could pass for a knight. Surely marrying Jonathan Alison was better than being murdered in the woods. This was all my father's fault. I would still be home and safe if he hadn't gotten himself killed!

I groaned and crumbled to the forest floor. Finally, the tears came. Hidden in the shadow of the trees, I let myself cry.

I lay there for some time, not wanting to move, not wanting to face what lay ahead. A snort roused me. Warm breath on my hair. When I looked up again, the forest had grown darker. I pushed Snowfoot's head away and wiped my face. Snowfoot's black eyes followed me, asking what was next. I looked at the road and sighed.

"Not that way," I said. Then I took Snowfoot's reins, and together we trekked deeper into the forest.

The thick canopy of leaves blocked the sun. Snowfoot and I trudged side by side through the darkness with no idea what lay ahead. Just when I thought the forest would go on forever, faint daylight streamed in, and the trees parted. I emerged from the forest to find a farm surrounded by rolling green hills. The thatched-roof farmhouse was old but well kept. The barn beside it stood high on straight walls. A dirt path ran from the house's front door down to a garden. Beyond the garden was an expansive corral that held a single black horse.

Snowfoot tugged at his reins, pulling me forward.

"Whoa, boy," I called, planting my feet.

He snorted and nodded toward an apple tree at the base of the garden. My stomach grumbled at the sight of the fruit, even though it was still green on the tree.

"Fine," I said. "But we must be quick."

The horse in the corral watched us. It was a war horse, a mighty courser, black as pitch. It whinnied and broke into a run, circling the corral in powerful strides.

We reached the tree, and I plucked an apple and held it out

to Snowfoot with a flat hand. He took it in one bite. I picked another for myself. My teeth barely penetrated the apple's hard skin. I winced at the tart taste. I tried a second bite, then handed the apple to Snowfoot.

"Those won't be ripe for some time," a voice called.

I spun around in surprise, having not heard anyone approach. A hulking figure stood at the end of the path that led up to the house. Dirt stained the man's shirt and pants. His skin was tan, and his grey hair shined like polished steel. I felt vulnerable under the piercing gaze of his blue-grey eyes, as if he could see through me. I tensed, ready to flee, but the old man made no move forward. He was calm, almost as if he'd expected me.

"Your horse doesn't seem to mind the taste," he said.

The tree shook as Snowfoot tore another apple free.

"Snowfoot, enough." I pulled at his reins, but Snowfoot chomped stubbornly. "Forgive me," I stammered. "I didn't mean to trespass. We lost our way in the forest."

"Snowfoot," the farmer said. He nodded to the horse's feet. "I thought jousters were superstitious."

"What?"

The farmer's eyes fell upon the armor and lance on Snowfoot's back.

"I'm not superstitious," I said. "And I've yet to see a duel decided by the color of a horse's feet."

The farmer studied me. His expression wasn't mocking, simply curious.

"The armor belongs to my father," I explained. "He's here to compete in the Tournament of Champions."

"And what is that?"

"You don't know? Your King's tournament will be held but an hour's ride from here."

The man shrugged. "I keep to my farm."

"It is the biggest jousting tournament in history."

"It must be to bring a Scottish knight onto English soil."

"Not only Scots. Knights from all over Europe are coming to compete for the title."

The farmer rubbed his short grey beard. "Your father is a knight, then."

"His name is Sir William Kay."

"And you have his armor."

"I'm bringing it to him in York," I said. "I'm his squire."

The man raised an eyebrow. "Is it common to have female squires in Scotland?"

"My father values talent over tradition."

"Your father sounds like a wise man."

"He was—he is."

The farmer studied me again. Then his eyes moved to the forest. For a second, I feared the riders had followed me. But there was no movement except for the quivering leaves.

"Are you in trouble, girl?" the farmer asked.

"No." I looked away from the farmer's gaze. He stepped forward, and I tensed. Though grey of head, he was solidly built with the thick arms of one who spent his days working the fields. He stopped before Snowfoot and extended a massive hand.

"I'd be careful," I warned. "Snowfoot doesn't take kindly to strangers."

"He seems friendly enough to me," the farmer said, rubbing Snowfoot's mane. Snowfoot snorted and nodded his appreciation. "You have nothing to fear from me, girl. You and your horse are welcome to as many apples as you like. There are riper things in the garden if you prefer—"

"Thank you, but I must be going. My father is expecting me in York."

The farmer started to speak and then stopped. "I understand." He gave Snowfoot one last pat and stepped away. "But take caution. These are dangerous roads to travel at night. Even for a squire."

I nodded and pulled Snowfoot's reins. This time, the horse obeyed. The last glow of sunlight was fading behind the mountains. I shivered as we entered the dark forest. After days of travel, I'd finally reached the outskirts of York—but it didn't matter. I had no money for an inn. These woods would be my home tonight.

Unless...

I stopped and hunched behind the bushes at the edge of the forest, watching the farmhouse. After a couple of hours, the light in the window finally went out, and I crept from my hiding place in the trees. My heart raced as Snowfoot and I made our way across the farmer's land. A rumble of hooves shook the ground and stopped my breath. Somewhere in the darkness, the black courser ran in its corral.

I reached the barn and pulled Snowfoot inside, closing the creaking door behind us. I listened for noise from the house, but nothing came. It was dark inside the barn, but Snowfoot found some hay, and the barn soon filled with the sound of hungry chomping. I stumbled toward him and managed to strip off his saddle in the darkness. Then I curled up on a bed of hay in the corner of the barn.

I didn't know how I was going to survive until the Tournament of Champions, but I was too tired to worry. For tonight, at least, I had a roof over my head. I pulled my travel cloak tight and fell asleep.

Life has always felt like a series of accidents, a messy collision of will and chance. But looking back now, I can see traces of a path, winding though it is. I have no other explanation for how I happened upon that farm, the one place in all the world that could change my stars.

A Discovery

I woke with a start. Daylight seeped in through the barn walls. I'd slept the whole night.

"Come on, Snowfoot," I called, scrambling to my feet, pulling the hay from my hair. But as I reached to the wall for support, I felt a stab of pain and jerked my hand away. I gaped at the collection of rusted weapons before me: swords, shields, maces, axes, and war lances. This was no farmer's barn.

A heavy chest lay in the corner, half-covered by hay. I crossed to the chest and pulled at the lid, straining against its rusted hinges. The lid creaked open, revealing grey armor. An eye on the side of a figurine gazed up from within the chest. I pushed the chain mail aside to find a metal bird. I seized the hand-sized bird and pulled it from the chest. A chill swept through me as I saw what I was holding: a screeching grey eagle adorning the top of a knight's helmet.

Impossible!

I stuffed the helmet back into the chest and closed the lid. I raced across the barn and saddled Snowfoot. The horse snorted when I set my father's armor on his back.

"Quiet," I said and grabbed his reins. "We're getting out of here."

I opened the barn door and froze. A bucket of water and a bowl of porridge lay on the ground before me. I stared at the offering. Before I could stop him, Snowfoot pushed forward and started lapping up water from the bucket.

I stepped out of the doorway and peered around the edge of the barn. The farmer was down the hill, working in the garden. My mind told me to run, to bolt for the trees and disappear into the forest. But hunger got the better of me. I picked up the bowl and devoured the warm porridge.

When I'd finished, I looked again at the man in the garden, judging the figure against all the stories I'd been told. Could it really be him?

I had to know.

I left Snowfoot and walked down the hill to the garden.

If the farmer was surprised to see me, he didn't show it. He continued hoeing as if I wasn't there. I stood at the edge of the garden, seeing the old man's broad frame in a new light.

"Thank you for the breakfast," I said.

"You're welcome," he said without looking up.

After a minute of silence, I decided to be direct. "I saw the weapons in your barn. Where did you get them?"

The farmer continued his work, digging up the earth with powerful strokes. "Those are just old tools I've no more use for," he said.

Though he dressed like a farmer, there was something about his demeanor, a certain poise in the way he moved and carried himself that showed through his tattered clothes and dirt-stained skin. I could imagine him before his grey hair, shielded in armor, slaying my countrymen with a lance.

"You're him, aren't you?" I said. "The Grey Knight."

The hoe caught in the ground, a moment's hesitation before the farmer continued turning the dark soil. "My name is Gowyn," he said.

"I saw the eagle helmet," I said, my voice rising. "Tell me the truth!"

Gowyn stopped hoeing. He looked at me with those sharp, blue-grey eyes. "The truth? And that's what you've told me, is it? Your father is waiting in York while you travel alone with a fortune in armor?"

I bit my lip and looked away. The land was quiet; the forest surrounding the lonely farm cut it off from the outside world. Somehow, against all odds, I'd stumbled upon the home of the greatest jouster of all time. It had to be for a reason.

"My father is not waiting for me in York," I said. "He's dead. I've come to take his place in the Tournament of Champions."

The flat head of the hoe stopped in the dirt. Gowyn raised an eyebrow and studied me. "Then you're in even more trouble than I thought, girl."

"I'm not a little girl. I'm a jouster."

This time I met Gowyn's gaze and held it.

"I'm sorry about your father," he said at last. "But it would be best for you to go home and forget about the tournament."

"I can't."

Gowyn leaned on his hoe. "Whatever you're running away from won't be solved with a trophy. And you bring no honor to your father by joining him in death."

"My father believed that we all have a path to follow. It wasn't an accident that brought me here. I was sent to you, the Grey Knight, for a purpose."

"My name is Gowyn. And you came here by chance, that is all."

I stepped forward. "You must train me. I can't win the tournament on my own."

"I'm sorry. That's not possible."

"Please, Sir Gowyn. I'm a hard worker. You won't find me a burden, I promise."

"You don't understand—"

"I have nowhere else to go," I said, my voice breaking.

Gowyn looked to the sky. "Why must trouble always find me?" He uttered a long, tired sigh. "Fine. You can stay here for now."

"Thank you, sir! I won't—"

He raised a hand, cutting me off.

"But I cannot train you. I'm done fighting."

I wanted to tell him he was wrong—jousting wasn't fighting; it was a beautiful, artful sport that I'd loved since I learned to ride. But for once, I held my tongue. "Thank you, Sir Gowyn," I said with a bow.

He held up his hand again. "Gowyn will do."

"Gowyn," I repeated. "My name is Meridian Kay."

Gowyn grunted. "If you don't mind, Meridian, I have work to do." He went back to his hoeing as if ignoring me would make me disappear. I looked around, unsure what to do. In the corral, the black courser whose hoofbeats I'd heard racing throughout the night stood still as a statue, watching me. I turned from the horse back to Gowyn.

"Sir . . . rr . . . Gowyn. Would you mind if I took my horse through some exercises?"

"You're free to do as you please," he said without looking up.

"Thank you." I walked back to the barn, my steps suddenly lighter. Not only did I have a roof over my head, I had a place to practice.

I found Snowfoot in the barn, his head buried in hay. I removed the sack of armor from his back and took up the practice lance.

"Come on, you pig," I said, spinning the lance in my hands. "We have training to do."

Practicing to Practice

It was below the garden, on a patch of level ground, that I trained. I spent the morning running Snowfoot through a series of passes to improve his acceleration for the burst of speed required in jousting. It felt good to take my mind off my troubles and focus on jousting.

I was aware of Gowyn's eyes upon me. At first, he rarely glanced up from his work, but the longer I practiced, the more I caught him watching. I found myself pushing Snowfoot faster, wanting to show off my skill as a rider. It wasn't every day that you practiced in front of the legendary Grey Knight.

When riding practice was done, Snowfoot rested under the shade of the apple tree while I worked on my lance technique. I took a wide stance and held my lance tight to my right side. Then I shot the lance out, striking the open air. I repeated the movement again and again, making sure to cradle my elbow at my hip before extending in a powerful, straight line.

After countless strikes, I finished by knocking an apple off the tree with one perfect thrust. I lowered my lance and turned to see if Gowyn was watching. The old knight was at the nearby well, filling buckets with water, his face bent in a frown. I worried the old knight didn't approve of a girl jousting. Was he going to change his mind and make me leave?

Gowyn picked up the two buckets and walked toward the corral. I hurried over to him. "Here," I said, "let me help."

Gowyn allowed me to take a bucket, though he hadn't seemed burdened by the weight.

"Thank you again for letting me train," I said, struggling to hold the bucket steady with two hands as water sloshed over the lid. "I can't tell you how good it feels to practice again."

"Is that what you were doing?" he said. "Practicing?"

I looked at him, confused. "Of course. What do you mean?"

Gowyn reached over the fence and poured his bucket of water into the horse's trough. The black courser stomped its feet and ran circles around the corral.

"Nothing," Gowyn said. "It's none of my business."

"What?" I stopped and set my bucket down. "Tell me."

Gowyn turned. "You're practicing to practice, not to compete."

"What do you mean?" I asked. He'd seen me practice dozens of passes and work on my lance technique until I could hardly lift my arm.

"An archer doesn't spend the day plucking an empty bowstring—he shoots arrows. Skills are specific. You get better at what you spend your time doing. What you were doing wasn't jousting."

"Well, I don't have an opponent."

"That's true, but there's still an enormous gap between what you were practicing and what you'll face in an actual tournament."

I scoffed. "You make it sound like I've wasted these hours of practice."

He walked toward me and picked up the second bucket in his free hand. "You work hard, Meridian."

"But?"

"But there is a better way to practice."

"Then show me."

Gowyn poured the second bucket into the trough. Then he met my gaze. With a sigh, he walked up the hill and disappeared into the barn. A minute later, he emerged carrying a rope and a piece of metal. I followed him down the path to where I'd been training.

"First, you should always be riding," he said. "The only time you're off your horse in jousting is when you've lost."

We reached the flat of land and Gowyn flung the rope over a high branch of the apple tree.

"Second, strike an actual target." He tied the rope around the piece of metal. "You need power and accuracy to unhorse an opponent."

"But that's your armor!" I said, staring at the eagle emblem engraved on the breastplate.

Gowyn nodded to the dangling breastplate. "A true strike will dent metal." Then he turned and walked up the hill without another word.

After he'd disappeared into the house, I studied the breastplate of the Grey Knight. "Come on, Snowfoot," I said, picking up the practice lance. "Let's show him what we can do."

In all my solo practice at home, I'd focused on hitting my target, not on what hitting that target would lead to. In competition, more points were awarded for breaking a lance on an opponent than for a simple strike, and unhorsing an opponent was an automatic victory. As I'd mostly practiced catching rings, I never developed power. The weakness in my training became clear as I struck the breastplate pass after pass without leaving so much as a scratch.

The morning's joy of jousting gave way to frustration and failure. I changed my strategy, pushing Snowfoot faster to gather more momentum. I found the closer I rode to the target, the more power I could generate from my strike; and where before I'd used only my arm, I was now throwing my whole body into the blows.

Snowfoot's pace slowed as the day wore on, but I kept pushing. I refused to surrender to the Grey Knight's challenge. I attacked the breastplate over and over until the light faded, and, trying to raise my lance, I collapsed out of the saddle.

When I woke, I was lying on a cot. Lantern light illuminated the humble furnishings of Gowyn's house. I tried to push myself up, but my arm buckled, and I fell back down.

Gowyn walked from the kitchen, carrying a bowl and a cup of water. He handed me the water, and I drank it gratefully. The liquid was like an elixir. I realized with sudden embarrassment that I must have passed out, and Gowyn had carried me up to the house. I'd wanted to prove my skill so badly but had only made a fool of myself.

"Here." Gowyn took the cup and handed me the bowl.

"Thank you," I muttered. I set the bowl on my chest and tried to lift the spoon. I winced and then switched to my left hand. It was a simple vegetable stew, but at that moment, it was the most delicious meal in the world.

The old knight sat in a chair, watching me eat. When I finished, he offered me a second bowl, and I devoured that as well.

"That was a foolish thing you did today," Gowyn said when I'd scraped the bowl clean. "You're lucky you didn't get trampled."

"Snowfoot would never hurt me," I said.

He studied me for a moment. "You have determination, I'll

give you that." He bent down and lifted something that scraped the floor. "And determination can get you far."

He set the breastplate beside me. I studied the metal in the lantern light. At the bottom, just below the eagle's talons, was a tiny dent. I ran my finger over the mark that had taken me all day to make.

"But determination alone won't get you through a tournament," Gowyn said.

"I know. That's why you have to teach me."

Gowyn shook his head. "I told you, I can't."

I pulled myself to a sitting position. "Why won't you train me? You don't think I should joust because I'm a girl, is that it? You think I'm dishonoring your precious knighthood?"

"I've seen too many ways a knight can bring dishonor to his title," Gowyn said. "Pursuing a dream is not one of them."

"Then why won't you teach me?"

"Because this sport is dangerous. I've seen the lives it's taken. Trust me, Meridian, any glory earned is fleeting. In the end, all you're left with is pain."

A shadow seemed to cross his face. What had happened to the great Grey Knight to make him disappear and live out his days alone?

"I know it's dangerous," I said. "I know I have almost no chance of winning. But I love jousting. And I'm good at it. And my father . . . he would've . . ." My voice broke, and I bit down, refusing to cry. Taking a deep breath, I met Gowyn's eyes. "I'm going to compete in the Tournament of Champions. I know it sounds crazy, but I have to do it."

"It is crazy," Gowyn said after a long pause. "But noble goals often are."

My pulse quickened at this crack in his armor. "Then you think I should do it?"

"No, I think you should ride straight home. But it's not for me to say. It's your heart you must answer to."

"My mother says my heart is what gets me into trouble."

"Trouble finds us, regardless. Sometimes it's better to choose the trouble we face."

I thought of my father and what chasing his dream had cost him. If he'd put away his lance, he would still be alive. But would he be happy? Would I?

"What you said today, about practicing to compete rather than practicing to practice. Are there more principles like that?"

"There are."

"Will you teach me?"

Gowyn ran a hand through his grey hair. "You won't give up, will you?"

"No."

"I should have sent you back into the forest the moment I saw you and that unlucky horse of yours." He shook his head, but the corners of his mouth revealed the faintest hint of a smile. "All right, I will show you a few things. I don't know about winning the tournament, but maybe we can keep you from getting your skull caved in."

I shouted with delight. "Thank you, Gowyn! I'll work hard. I promise. I'll do whatever you say without question."

"If you have a question, you better ask it."

I smiled. "What do we do first?"

"First, get some rest."

Gowyn helped me to the barn. He set up the cot in the corner and left me a lantern. "Get some sleep," he said. "Training starts in the morning, and we can't have you falling off your horse again."

When Gowyn left, I was too excited to sleep. The events of the past few days swirled around in my head. Since my father's death, I'd been on the run, hungry, penniless, and alone in a strange land. Now, I'd found not only a place to stay but the one teacher who could prepare me for the Tournament of Champions. I couldn't wait to start training.

It felt as if my head had just touched the pillow when I was awoken by the sound of hammering.

Moving Target

It couldn't possibly be morning already; the barn was still dark. But the banging noise continued. I struggled out of bed and began to dress. This proved difficult, as I couldn't lift my arms over my head, but my excitement overcame my soreness. Today, I would train with the legendary Grey Knight. I pulled on my boots and hurried outside.

In the predawn light, I found the source of the awful noise. Gowyn stood over a mess of boards and wagon wheels, hammering away.

"You're getting an early start," I said, unable to make out what farm project he was working on. "Do you need any help?"

Gowyn drove a nail into a board and looked up. "There's breakfast in the house. Best get something in you before you start."

I smiled with relief; he still meant to train me. I rushed to the house and made quick work of the porridge, then hurried back to the barn and saddled Snowfoot. When I emerged, Gowyn was still at work. I waited as he finished sawing a plank in two.

"I'm ready," I said.

Gowyn set his tools down and started down the hill. I pulled Snowfoot after him, excited to see what training awaited.

"You've shown you have the drive," Gowyn said. "But to become great, you must couple that drive with better practice, training the skills you will use in competition." Gowyn stopped before the apple tree where the breastplate hung once again. "Unfortunately, secrecy prevents you from training against live opponents, but you can still take steps to better replicate a duel."

"What steps?" I asked.

"In a joust, your opponent doesn't stand still, waiting for you to attack." He pushed the breastplate. It swung through the air in a twisting pattern. "Let's see how you fare against a moving target."

I took up my lance and mounted Snowfoot. "Come on, boy."

I rode to the end of the track and raised my spear, signaling I was ready. Gowyn pushed the breastplate again. "Yah!" Snowfoot took off, and I focused on the swaying target, gauging my approach. I lowered my lance and cradled it against my side, aiming. But as Snowfoot drew near, the breastplate twisted away from me. I drove my lance forward, missing the dancing target by a foot.

"Let me try again," I said, turning Snowfoot around before Gowyn could say anything.

Once more, Gowyn pushed the breastplate, but this time in a new direction. Snowfoot charged toward the apple tree, and I drove him toward the center of the rope this time, adjusting for movement in either direction. I concentrated on the target, seeing nothing else. I struck out, just missing the breastplate as it spun out of my lance's path.

Snowfoot slowed to a stop, and I threw the reins down. My

first challenge, and I'd failed miserably. Gowyn walked over, and I braced myself for his criticism.

"You were closer that time," he said.

"I still missed."

"It was an improvement."

I was taken aback by Gowyn's calm, matter-of-fact tone. "Why aren't you mad or disappointed?" I asked, unable to hold back the quiver in my voice. "I'm training for the Tournament of Champions, and I can't even hit a breastplate."

"You don't have to prove yourself to me, Meridian. You're here to put in the work and get better. You started training yesterday so comfortable with your task, you might as well have been riding with your eyes closed. But this time, you were challenged. This time, you made adjustments as you would in competition."

"I still failed."

"What will you do differently on the next pass?"

I glanced back to the breastplate swaying at the end of the rope. I thought through my previous passes, looking for information. I pictured the breastplate's jerky path as it danced just out of reach.

"I won't strike where the target *is*," I said. "I'll strike where it *will be*."

Gowyn handed me the reins. "Let's see it."

I set off for another pass. Once again, Gowyn swung the breastplate. This time, I focused not on the spinning sheet of metal. I focused on its path, predicting where it would move next. As I drew close and thrust my lance, the breastplate twisted. I struck at its thin side; the lance grazed its edge.

I made several more passes. Each pass, Gowyn moved the breastplate in a new arc, sometimes spinning it side to side, sometimes sending it forward and back. Finally, after a series of partial hits, the breastplate swung open, and I struck its center with a satisfying clang.

"I did it!" I exclaimed so loud you'd think I'd won a tournament.

Gowyn nodded. "How did you do it?"

"Luck, I guess. The target opened at the right time."

"Luck didn't hit a moving target, Meridian. You did. What did you notice about that pass?"

I thought about it for a moment. It had felt like the previous passes. Was there something to learn from it?

"I waited," I said. "Instead of striking out when distance demanded, I waited a moment longer, until the breastplate spun open."

"That took patience and focus," Gowyn said. "A moment can make all the difference."

"What now?" I asked.

"Now you couple accuracy with power. Swing the target before you start each pass. Come find me when you've added a second dent."

"You're leaving?"

"I have work to finish."

With that, Gowyn walked up the hill. A moment later, the sound of hammering filled the air. Though left alone, I continued training, spinning the breastplate before each pass. Striking the moving target proved difficult and hitting it square enough to dent the thick metal nearly impossible. It was past noon before the accumulation of strikes had led to a second dent on the breastplate. I dismounted Snowfoot and walked up the hill to report to Gowyn.

Gowyn was still hard at work. His project now stood over head height. It looked like he was building a gallows.

"I've dented it," I said.

"And how did you do that?" Gowyn asked without looking up from his work.

"I hit it hard over and over," I said dryly.

"That's a good strategy."

"Is this what you call teaching?" I demanded. "I thought you were going to prepare me for the Tournament of Champions. If you're too busy tinkering on your farm equipment to help, just say so."

Gowyn stopped hammering and ran a hand through his grey beard. He set his hammer down and grabbed one end of a thick log. "Help me lift this," he said.

I sighed and walked over and grabbed the other end. We heaved the log overhead, my sore right arm trembled under the weight. Together, we set the log into a groove atop a center post. Gowyn climbed atop the structure and nailed the log in place. When he was done, he climbed down and stepped back to examine his work. Four wheels were set around a wide base, out of which rose a post. Another wheel lay flat atop the post. The log we'd just attached sat above the wheel, its arms extending horizontally like a cross. At the end of one arm hung a rope. At the end of the other arm, wooden boards were carved into the shape of a two-sided shield.

"What is it?" I asked.

"It's called a quintain," Gowyn said. "It's a training device for jousting."

I gaped at the contraption. "You built this for me?"

"It's not an opponent," Gowyn said, wiping his brow. "But it's better than hitting targets at the end of a rope. Now, let's see if we can move it."

Together we pushed the heavy quintain down the hill. I couldn't believe he'd spent the day building a training device. I felt ashamed for doubting him.

We stopped at the bottom of the hill and positioned the

quintain in the center of the track. Gowyn spun the horizontal wagon wheel, adjusting the crossbar until the shield arm lay over the track. To the end of the other arm, he tied a bag of sand.

"What's the sand for?" I asked.

"Counterbalance," Gowyn said. "You'll have to strike the shield hard and true to move it. Plus, it will serve as a teacher."

"A teacher?"

"You'll see."

I mounted Snowfoot and rode to the end of the dirt track, excited to use the new contraption.

"Are you ready?" Gowyn called.

I took a moment, gathering my courage, for the quintain looked like a torture device. "Ready," I said at last.

My first pass at the quintain was tentative. I hadn't gained much speed by the time I rammed my lance into the shield. The arms of the quintain spun around, and the sandbag slammed into my back. I flew off Snowfoot and crashed to the ground, the air knocked from my lungs. I was still gasping for breath when Gowyn appeared above me.

"What was that?" I wheezed.

"A lesson."

Gowyn helped me to my feet. I dusted myself off. "Are you trying to kill me?"

"I'm preparing you."

"How am I supposed to practice with the sandbag hitting me?"

"Don't let it hit you." Gowyn spun the quintain's shield back into place. "Ready to go again?"

I looked at the heavy sandbag hanging from the back arm of the quintain. A "teacher," Gowyn had called it. I realized I'd been riding too slow. In competition, jousters rode to unhorse their opponents. The sandbag was to teach me to joust at speed.

I picked up my lance. "I'm ready."

The next pass I rode as fast as I could, the sting of the saddlebag still fresh in my mind. But this time my lance went wide, striking only the edge of the shield and hardly moving it. The quintain was proving difficult. I needed to joust with power and accuracy.

"It looked like you were afraid of getting hit," Gowyn said. There was no judgment in his tone, but I still felt defensive.

"I'm not afraid," I said.

"It's helpful to train with fear. You'll face that feeling in the tournament."

"Practice for competition," I said, repeating Gowyn's phrase.

He nodded. "Practice for competition."

We continued through the afternoon. I'd ended enough passes on my back that I was now caked in dirt. And each time I found a rhythm, striking the shield while avoiding the sandbag, Gowyn would add some challenge to increase the difficulty, never allowing me to stay comfortable for long. I approached the quintain from different angles, different distances, each time adjusting to the new challenge while trying to hit the target with power and accuracy.

When, following yet another blow from the sandbag, I struggled to climb back in the saddle, Gowyn said we were done for the day. I sighed and wiped the dirt from my brow. "I understand if you don't want to train me anymore."

Gowyn looked surprised. "Why would you think that?"

"I was awful today. Again and again, I failed to hit the target."

"I made mistakes, too," Gowyn said. "Mistakes are necessary. Practice isn't about looking good, it's about improving. It's about challenging yourself and stretching beyond what you think you're capable of. That is how you grow, Meridian."

"Then we must be doing it right because jousting has never felt this hard."

Gowyn smiled. "Challenges make us stronger."

I rubbed my aching shoulder. "I don't feel strong."

"No." Gowyn chuckled. "Probably not right now. But our goal is to be better tomorrow than we were today."

I grabbed Snowfoot's reins and started up the long path to the house. As I passed near him, the black horse whinnied and galloped around the corral. I stopped and watched his powerful, wild movements as the sun disappeared behind the mountains. I'd started the day excited to train. Now I felt tired and discouraged. Practice had made me better, but it also showed me my limitations. How could I possibly compete in the Tournament of Champions against the world's greatest jousters?

Three-Foot World

I struggled to sleep that night as tournament scenarios played out in my mind: embarrassing myself in front of thousands of people, disgracing my father's name, being discovered as an impostor, getting injured or even killed. The next morning, I didn't want to get out of bed. My body was sore, but it was the sudden doubt that held me in place. Gowyn had explained that mistakes were necessary, but that didn't change how I felt. I'd always believed I was a gifted jouster who would succeed if only given the chance. But yesterday's training had made it clear how far behind I really was. Did I really have it in me to be great?

Gowyn must have sensed something was wrong. Before starting our morning practice, he sent me to chop firewood. The task, which I'd seen our workers back home perform, proved harder than expected. The axe head stuck in the logs constantly, and I spent as much time prying the blade loose as chopping wood. My frustration grew as thoughts of the tournament filled my head once again. I'd been crazy to think I could compete with the top knights in Europe.

I was thrown from these thoughts when a careless swing missed the log completely, and the axe blade came within inches of my foot. I jumped back and fell to the ground. Shaken by my near accident, I looked up to see Gowyn watching.

"Are you all right?" he asked.

"Fine." I stood and dusted off my pants. "I just got distracted."

"Where did your mind go?"

"I was thinking about the tournament."

Gowyn picked up the axe. The heavy tool seemed light in his hand. "This is a useful tool, but it can be dangerous if you're not paying attention." It was as if my father were there, speaking to me through Gowyn. *Keep your head and your feet in the same place, Meridian. When you're chopping wood, chop wood!*

Gowyn held out the axe, but I didn't take it.

"I can't do this," I said. "There's no point in training."

"You said you loved jousting."

"That's when I thought I was good at it. Now I know I was only fooling myself."

Gowyn lowered the axe head to the ground. "When was the first time you jousted?"

I thought back to the day we returned from a tournament in Edinburgh. "I was six," I said. "I begged my father to take me jousting. I rode on his horse with him, jousting against the practice post, trying to catch rings."

"And did you catch a lot of rings?"

"No. I shrieked every time the horse took off. I could barely keep my eyes open." I smiled at the memory: sitting in the front of his saddle, my father guiding my hands, laughing at my screams, giving me the reins to lead us back home.

"So how did you get better?" Gowyn asked.

"I got stronger and learned to ride. I practiced."

Gowyn nodded. "And how will you be better tomorrow than today?"

"By practicing." I sighed. "But I don't see the point. The

Tournament of Champions is only a couple months away. And if I lose, I won't just fail my family and dishonor my father's name. I could be imprisoned for impersonating a knight!"

"That's a lot to take on. I can see why you'd be distracted." Gowyn rubbed his beard, thinking, and then said, "Reach your arms out, Meridian."

"What? Why?"

"How far can you reach?"

I reached my arms out in front of me and then to the sides, stretching my fingers.

"About three feet," Gowyn said. "That is all that is within your reach in a given moment. That is what you can influence. That is where you focus your attention. The tournament, your opponents, the crowd, how you'll finish, those things are beyond your circle of control. So, stay in your three-foot world."

"But what will that do? This tournament is too big. I have no chance of winning."

Gowyn sat down and motioned for me to join him. Then he told me a story. "There once was a mountain on the outskirts of a small village. One day, a man set out to climb the mountain. The villagers that heard about his plan called him a fool, for everyone could see the mountain was too high and steep to climb. But ever since he was a boy, the man had looked at the great mountain outside his village and imagined what it would be like to reach the top. Where others saw impossibility, he saw a challenge. So, the man ignored the warnings of the other villagers and, at first light, he began to climb the mountain. He was not an exceptional climber. He had no special tools. Climbing was slow, for the face was steep. Many times the man thought of turning back, for the undertaking did seem impossible. But each time, he convinced himself to climb just another few feet. He could have worried about what the villagers would say if he failed. He could have worried about the many treacherous stretches of rock that still lay ahead. He could have worried about the ground hundreds of feet below him, and how one mistake could cost him his life. Instead, he only focused on what he could reach at that moment. The next handhold, the next step. He stayed within his three-foot world. Eventually, those three feet added up, and he reached the top of the mountain."

Gowyn put his hand on my shoulder. "What you're trying to do might seem impossible from where you are, Meridian. But you don't have to conquer it in one leap. Stay inside your three-foot world. The steps might feel small. They might feel slow. But you can climb a mountain that way."

Gowyn left me to finish my work. After sitting for a few minutes, I set the log back on the stump and picked up the axe. I let go of thoughts of jousting and the Tournament of Champions, of my family's debts and reputation, even of the stacks of wood yet to chop. Instead, I felt the weight of the axe in my hand and the smooth wood of the handle.

Three feet, I told myself, letting go of everything outside my circle. I focused on the log before me, on the crack in the wood's swirling grain. Then I raised the axe and brought it down on that point, splitting the log in two.

The Two Mindsets

The Tournament of Champions still loomed before me, but I was now committed to the process, focusing on what I could accomplish in my three-foot world. And as a teacher, Gowyn proved just as committed.

He was a champion knight whose feats were legendary, yet he taught with patience and humility. Practices were demanding, but he never barked orders or grew angry at my mistakes. Instead, he taught with questions, guiding me to explore and find my own solutions. If I got stuck on a task, he'd nudge me with an observation or a suggestion.

After practice, we would reflect on the day's training. He'd have me take the lead, noting what I did well and what I could improve upon next time. When I'd focus too much on the negative, as I had a habit of doing, Gowyn would encourage me to find positives. "It's easy to spot mistakes and get discouraged," he'd say. "It's important to *hunt the good stuff*."

After a week of training, my jousting had improved tremendously. I struck the quintain's shield with more power and consistency, riding fast enough that the sandbag was no longer a cause for worry.

It was around this point that my growth seemed to plateau. It became difficult to make changes, and I struggled to make changes in my technique. I was harder on myself in practice—hitting the target was no longer enough. If I was to win the Tournament of Champions, I needed to be perfect.

As I rode toward the quintain, I went through the checklist in my head: steer Snowfoot on course and at the right speed, lower the lance into position, hold the angle with my right elbow high and steady. But when I performed the pass, my technique faltered, and I struck the edge of the shield.

"You seem frustrated," Gowyn said as I climbed off Snowfoot.

"I still can't get it right," I said.

"Get what right?"

I threw up my hands. "Anything. If it's not my angle, it's my lean. If it's not my distance, it's my thrust."

Gowyn listened to me complain. "Jousting is hard," he agreed. "It challenges the mind as well as the body."

I grimaced. My father always said I had good skills but lacked mental strength. Gowyn seemed to sense my frustration. "Your skills have come a long way in the last week, Meridian. I think it's time to practice the trusting mindset."

"The what?"

Gowyn stepped closer and petted Snowfoot's mane. "A mindset is a way of thinking, an attitude. In practice, there are two mindsets at play: the training mindset and the trusting mindset. The training mindset is used to acquire skill. It is the mindset for developing a specific technique, for evaluating a pass critically, for fixing mistakes."

"That's what I'm doing."

Gowyn nodded. "Yes, and the training mindset is important, especially as you're developing a new skill. But it is not the mindset you'll use in competition."

Seeing my confusion, Gowyn continued. "The trusting mindset is used to let skills out. It is the mindset for riding free and with conviction. It doesn't judge. It accepts. While the training mindset seeks to make things happen, the trusting mindset lets things happen. It is important to balance both the training and the trusting mindsets in practice, but it is with the trusting mindset you will compete."

"I'm supposed to stop thinking?"

Gowyn raised an eyebrow, and I felt embarrassed at my tone. Over our time together, I'd learned to hold back my initial impulse to snap at him. For the most part.

"What do you think about when you perform a pass?" he asked.

I rattled off my checklist, explaining some things I focus on: my horse, my eyeline, the position of my arm and shield, the angle of my lance, my breathing.

"That's a lot to carry in your mind," he said. "You think you can focus on all of those things at the same time during a pass?"

"No, I guess not," I said. "So, I'm supposed to forget about technique during a tournament?"

"Technique is important, but it is developed in practice. Competition is not the time to worry about the position of your arm or whether your angle is perfect. You compete your best when you trust your training and ride free."

Gowyn let go of Snowfoot's mane and stepped back. "If you want to work on a specific technique and stay in the training mindset, then do so. But this is how you have spent all your practices thus far. You must develop the trusting mindset as well. Just as a knight wouldn't rely on a sword he's never sharpened, you must hone the trusting mindset in order for it to hold up under the pressures of competition. To be a champion, a knight must practice the trusting mindset."

I wiped sweat from my brow, trying to understand the two

mindsets. "I see how you work on a training mindset skill such as power or lance work, but how do you practice the trusting mindset?"

"Think about when you joust. What are you like when you're at your best?"

I thought for a moment, remembering the hours spent on my home practice grounds, catching rings, jousting against my father. Then I thought through my training with Gowyn, the passes where I'd hit the target true, when jousting felt easy.

"I wasn't worried about making mistakes," I said. "I was focused . . . and determined to win."

"And what did it feel like to ride?"

I met Snowfoot's eyes and smiled. "I felt free."

"It doesn't sound like you were worried about technique. You focused on your target and trusted yourself. You rode free."

"Yes."

Gowyn nodded at the quintain. "Before you make this next pass, take a moment to clear away the thoughts, judgments, and doubts that want to fill your head. Simply focus on your target and trust yourself. Just joust."

"That's it?"

"You may find it more difficult than you think."

I climbed back on Snowfoot and turned him around. Was Gowyn right? Had I been overthinking? Was chasing perfect technique actually costing my performance? I decided to let go of my thoughts and simply trust.

This proved impossible.

I ran a series of passes and each time thoughts were there, reminding me what I was doing wrong. I was still out of rhythm, failing to hit the center of the shield. Gowyn observed without comment. After a while, he stopped me to ask what I noticed.

"I keep losing control on my approach," I said. "And my lance arm isn't locking in position."

Gowyn nodded and told me to stay there as he walked up to the barn. He came back down the hill carrying a rope. He tied one end of the rope around my waist. The other end, he tied to the quintain's post.

"All right, go again," he said.

"What? I can't. I'm tied to the quintain!"

"That makes it hard to perform, doesn't it? But that's what you've been doing. Trying to joust while carrying the last pass with you."

Gowyn drew a knife from his belt. "Learn what you can. Make adjustments. Then . . ." He cut the rope, releasing me. "Let go and move on."

I sighed and pulled the rope off me. "But how do I let go of the last pass? How do I turn off my thoughts?"

"You can't turn off your thoughts," Gowyn said. "But you can aim your attention. Focus on one thing—the target or your next task. It takes practice like any other skill. Under pressure, a knight's dominant habit will emerge. You've spent your life practicing the training mindset, so that is what you joust with. Now you must develop your trusting mindset."

I led Snowfoot down the track to try again. However, this time I didn't rush into the pass. I took a moment to breathe. The thoughts were still there, swarming around my head like hornets, but I slowly directed my focus to the quintain's shield. When I felt my mind quiet, I took off.

Using this routine, I practiced the trusting mindset the rest of the afternoon. Gowyn never once mentioned my technique. Instead, he'd offer a quick thought or observation on trusting skill:

"How present were you on that pass?"

"You looked more aggressive there."

"It looked like you let go of the last pass and came back with conviction!"

Slowly, after enough passes, the burden of perfection began to melt away. I stopped worrying about what my body was doing; I simply jousted.

After practice, we sat down to reflect while Snowfoot grazed in the nearby grass.

"It felt different to joust like that," I said.

"It will feel different," Gowyn said. "It's a new habit you must train. Remember, you get better at what you spend your time doing. If you do one hundred passes tomorrow, at least sixty of them should be done with the trusting mindset. As the tournament draws nearer, the number should increase. Then, when you face down your opponents, you will be ready to trust and ride free."

Crossing the Board

Gowyn divided practice between the training and trusting mindsets, making it clear when I was to be "taking skills in" and when I was to be "letting skills out." Yet I still didn't fully understand the difference between the two mindsets. I asked Gowyn about the concept again.

"Follow me," he said and led me up the path to the barn. Once inside, he brought over a long wooden board and set it on the barn floor. "Walk across the board."

I looked at Gowyn, confused. The board was a full hand's width and lay flat on the ground.

Gowyn waited.

With a shrug, I stepped onto one end of the board and walked across with ease.

"How did you do that?" Gowyn asked when I'd finished.

"What do you mean? I just walked."

Gowyn nodded and picked the board off the ground. "Help me carry this."

Together we carried the board up the ladder to the hayloft. From there, Gowyn lifted the board overhead and slid it onto the barn's high rafters until it came to rest atop three widely spaced beams.

"Now," Gowyn said. "Walk across the board."

"What? That's like thirty feet off the ground."

Gowyn waited.

Not wanting to back down from his challenge, I climbed up into the barn's rafters, ducking under spider webs. From up there, it looked even higher. I clung to a rafter and waited for my legs to stop shaking.

"This is crazy," I said.

"You've already done it once."

"But that was on the ground, not from the top of a barn."

"It's the same board."

I took a deep breath and set my foot on the board. The plank of wood wobbled but held my weight. I took a deep breath and then let go of the rafters. I took a small step. The board tilted. My arms flailed out to the sides for balance. I took another step and was now suspended between two of the rafter beams. There was nothing to grab onto. If I fell, I would plummet all the way to the barn floor. Beads of sweat tickled my forehead, but I didn't dare wipe them for fear I'd lose my balance. I focused all my attention on my feet and not falling. My legs were stiff as I inched—heel over toe—across the board.

When I finally neared the end, I finished with a lunge and grabbed hold of the rafter. Panting, I stayed there, clinging to the beam until I could move again.

Gowyn offered me a hand down. Once I was safely on the ground, he asked, "What did you notice about the two times you walked across the board?"

"It was a lot harder the second time," I said, my heart finally slowing to a regular rhythm.

"What did you think about while you were crossing the second time?"

"Keeping my balance. Not falling off and breaking my neck!"

"And the first time?"

"The first time, I just walked."

"You just walked." Gowyn nodded. "When the board was on the ground, you didn't think about how to walk. You didn't worry about what your body was doing. Your movements were smooth and instinctual. All you focused on was getting to the end of the board.

"When you walked across the high board, your mind went to work. Your movements became slow and rigid. You were suddenly worried about the technique of walking. You didn't focus on your target at the end of the board, you focused on not falling off."

"Yes," I said, remembering the stiff, awkward way I shuffled across the board.

"That is the difference between the training and the trusting mindsets. There is a time to focus on skill and technique, but when it's time to perform, you must trust yourself. To compete with the trusting mindset is to walk across the high board as if it were on the ground."

"But how can I do that?" I asked. "It may be the same board, but the fall is real."

Gowyn smiled and put a hand on my shoulder. "You do it by practicing on the high board."

I looked up at the board suspended in the rafters high above. I didn't know if I could ever reach the point where I was jousting entirely on instinct, not worrying about being hit or falling. But I now had a clear picture of what the trusting mindset looked like.

I also knew it would be a while before I asked Gowyn for another demonstration.

Thinking Ground, Trusting Ground

I practiced the next morning, working on technique against the quintain. When I stopped to drink water, Gowyn approached.

"Your strikes are getting more accurate," he said.

"It feels better," I agreed, wiping my mouth and then holding the bucket of water up for Snowfoot.

"You've practiced with the training mindset. Now it's time to switch to the trusting mindset."

"But there's still a lot of technique I need to improve."

"Perhaps. But none so important as this skill." He tapped his temple. "You've developed a skill—now let it out. Go through your routine, focus on your target, and trust."

I remembered the feeling of walking across the high board, frozen by my thoughts. It was time to let go of thinking and practice trusting. I set the bucket down and mounted Snowfoot. We rode into position at the end of the track. Then I raised my lance and kicked Snowfoot. "Yah!"

I charged down the track toward the quintain. As I drew close, I dropped my lance into position and struck the shield, moving fast enough to avoid the swinging sandbag. Riding back, I evaluated my lance position and if I'd gotten enough power from my thrust.

"How was your conviction?" Gowyn asked.

"What?"

"On a scale of one to ten, how committed were you on your target versus worried about technique?"

"About a six," I admitted.

"What would it look like if you were a seven or eight?"

"I wouldn't care what my arm was doing. I'd focus on hitting the target."

Gowyn nodded. "Let's see you commit."

I reached the end of the track and turned around to start my pass, when Gowyn appeared in my path. I yelled in surprise and pulled Snowfoot's reins. "Whoa, boy!"

Gowyn raised a grey eyebrow. "Were you committed to your target or were you rushing?"

I sighed, embarrassed. I'd already forgotten.

"Don't begin a pass until you're fully committed," Gowyn said. "To perform your best, you must separate thinking from trusting."

"How do I do that?"

"It helps to come up with a reminder. What's a physical routine that will remind you to shift from thinking to trusting?"

I thought about taking three deep breaths, or not grabbing my reins until I was ready. But if I was going to remember to shift mindsets, the routine should be more external.

"What if I cross a line?"

"That would work." Gowyn picked up a stick and drew a line in the dirt in front of Snowfoot. "Think of the line as the border between thinking and trusting." He pointed to my side of the line. "That is your thinking ground. That is where you observe, plan, strategize, and make decisions. The thinking ground is important. It stops you from blindly rushing into a pass."

He tapped the dirt on the other side of the line.

"This is your trusting ground. This is where you let go of judgment and perform. Cross this line only once you're committed and ready to act. It's important to keep the trusting ground clean. If you ever find yourself about to make a pass and thoughts and doubts creep in, step back into the thinking ground. Take stock. Focus on one thing, then cross the line ready to attack."

I looked at the line as if it separated two worlds. How often had I rushed into a pass without thinking? Or how often had I ridden timidly because I was worried about my form? I could no longer afford to joust that way. For in a tournament, each pass could mean the difference between winning and losing, between life and death.

I waited in the thinking ground as thoughts on technique and cradling my elbow filled my head. When the thoughts began to clear, I took a few deep breaths and focused on the quintain's shield until everything else had faded away. Then I committed to one thing: *Be Aggressive*. Once committed, I grabbed the reins and stepped Snowfoot across the line onto the trusting ground.

"Yah!" I yelled. Snowfoot charged forward. I locked my eyes on the target and rode fast and aggressively. Nothing in the world mattered but the center of the shield. I punched the lance with all my strength. The lance struck true, cracking the wooden shield. I pulled Snowfoot to a stop beside the apple tree, unable to hide the smile on my face.

"How committed were you?" Gowyn asked.

"I was a ten," I said with pride.

"Why was it a ten?"

"I went through my routine and didn't step onto the

trusting ground until I was committed. I felt aggressive and free."

"Remember that feeling," Gowyn said. "And what it felt like to shift from thinking ground to trusting ground. Practice that, and it'll be with you in the tournament."

Exploring New Paths

The more I practiced the trusting mindset, the more my jousting improved. There were passes at the quintain when the judgmental voice would disappear, and I'd ride free. No longer focused on what my body was doing, I was able to concentrate outside myself and see the environment clearer. I'd catch Gowyn moving the shield arm at the last moment, and I'd adjust. The unpredictable became less of a surprise; I was jousting on instinct.

But after a few days, I found my strikes had grown increasingly wilder, my form undisciplined. I was improving on the mental side, but there were some technical skills I wanted to build. To my surprise, Gowyn agreed.

"It is good that you are focusing on the trusting mindset because that is where you need the most practice," Gowyn said. "But remember, it is a balance. Both mindsets are important."

I told him I wanted to practice with the training mindset and work on my technique.

"It's important to be specific and choose one focus," he said. "If you seek two destinations at once, you will reach neither."

"My lance control seems to be my biggest problem," I said. "I'm not locking it into position and holding it in line." This was part of my technique my father had always criticized: *A jouster must lock his elbow to his body in a cradle position in order to strike in a straight line, generating the most power and accuracy.* I'd been so focused on hitting the target my elbow wasn't locking, and my strike line was reckless.

At first, I wanted to practice without a target as I'd done at home, focusing on locking my elbow into the cradle over and over. But Gowyn reminded me I was "practicing to compete" and how it was important to train the whole movement to develop a skill.

So I jousted against the quintain, focusing on my lance control. Now that we were in the training mindset, Gowyn's questions moved from the outcome and tactics back to technique.

"What did you notice on that pass?" Gowyn asked.

"My lance was still unsteady," I said.

"What have you tried?"

"Locking my elbow tight to my body, but I'm still not getting it."

"Then try something else."

"But the cradle position is the correct form. I just need to hold my elbow closer for longer."

"And how is that working for you?" Gowyn asked. "Training is exploration. If one path is not working, explore another."

Gowyn stepped closer, rubbing his beard. "Try something for me. On the next pass, throw your elbow out as far from your body as you can. Like a chicken flapping its wing."

I shifted in my saddle. I could still hear my father's instructions on the right way to joust and yet Gowyn was telling me to do the opposite!

"Explore a different path," Gowyn said.

"All right." I sighed and started Snowfoot down the track. If the Grey Knight said to do something, it was worth a try.

"Like a chicken wing," Gowyn called.

I shook my head and slapped Snowfoot's reins. As we neared the quintain, I lowered my lance and tried to stick my elbow out, but as I neared the quintain, my habit took over, and I brought my arm tight for a normal pass.

"Was that a chicken wing?" Gowyn asked afterward.

"I couldn't do it," I said. "It felt too strange."

He scratched at his beard for a moment. Then he drew his knife and cut through the end of a rope. He tied the small piece of rope tightly around my elbow.

"Try moving the rope instead."

I looked at the rope on my elbow. "What's the difference?"

"The difference is the rope is outside your body. See how high you can raise the rope on this next pass."

I lifted my elbow into the chicken wing position, raising the rope to the sky.

Gowyn nodded. "Cluck, cluck."

I shook my head and turned Snowfoot to try again, intent on exaggerating the form to show Gowyn he was wrong. Snowfoot huffed and started down the track toward the quintain. This time when I lowered my lance, I flared out my arm, lifting the rope as high as I could. It felt ridiculous. My lance jumped all around, as if it were a snake in my hands. I jabbed weakly at the shield, missing my target by two feet.

I turned Snowfoot around, shaking my head as I approached Gowyn.

"What did you notice?" Gowyn asked.

"I couldn't get any power or control with my elbow that wide."

Gowyn nodded. "Now try a pass with the rope pulled back like you're giving someone behind you a black eye."

"What? That's even more ridiculous," I said. "My lance will be pointed at the ground."

Gowyn drew his elbow back as if he were striking someone behind him. "Black eye."

I turned Snowfoot for another pass. This time, I drove the rope back behind me. I had to twist my wrist to keep the lance from stabbing the ground and catapulting me from my saddle.

I thrust toward the shield, just clipping its edge, but still sending it spinning around. Wind rushed past as the sandbag whipped by the back of my head.

"What did you notice?" Gowyn asked.

"I still couldn't control the lance. I barely hit the shield."

"What else?"

I thought through the last pass. "I did have more power."

Gowyn nodded. "Now, extend the lance out far in front of you as if you're pointing the way."

"But I'll have no thrust."

Gowyn straightened his arm out in front of him. "Point the way."

I groaned but obeyed. Snowfoot charged at the quintain and this time, as I lowered my lance, I reached it out ahead of me, pointing at the shield. My shoulder burned, trying to hold the lance steady. As I came upon the quintain, I thrust, tapping the shield with no power.

I fumed as I rode back to Gowyn. "I noticed it was a waste of time," I said before he could even ask.

Gowyn nodded. "You didn't seem to have much power or control."

"Of course I didn't! What is the point of this? Instead of improving my form, I'm getting further away!"

Gowyn waited patiently. "One more pass," he said. He reached up and untied the rope from my arm. "This time, hold the lance as still as possible, as if it were a part of your body."

I took a breath and exhaled my frustration. Then I turned Snowfoot around for one more pass, happy to be done with Gowyn's games. I shook my elbow loose and looked down the track to the shield. My fingers tightened, gripping the handle. "Keep it still," I said.

Snowfoot galloped down the track. I focused not on my elbow but on holding the lance still as if it were a part of me. To my surprise, the lance tip barely moved. It stayed straight, locked on the shield. I thrust forward with all my strength, striking the center of the shield so hard the wood cracked on impact.

"It worked!" I said. "The lance felt steady. I held it in the cradle without even thinking about my elbow. How is that possible?"

"Earlier you did pass after pass with no adjustments," Gowyn said. "You thought you were making changes, but the changes were so tiny your body fell into its old habit. By exploring the extremes, you felt the full range, and it became easier to make a change.

"Sometimes when you're lost, you can find your way by first exploring all the paths that don't lead to your destination. And you may also find a new path."

"What do you mean?"

"Who determines the correct form for a jouster? If you unhorse your opponent, he will not ask whether your elbow was in line. Technique is not set in stone. Form changes to meet the demands of competition. Because no two jousts are the same, a knight must be a problem solver. Instead of scripting out your movement, you adapt to the situation and find a solution. For if you're convinced there is only one path to your destination, Meridian, what will you do when that road is blocked?"

Shadow

Practice had paid off. I was now holding the lance steadier, as if it were a part of my body. Plus, I found that driving my elbow back produced more power. Black eye indeed!

The better I got, the more Gowyn challenged me. Often, this wasn't in the form of instruction but a change in my task or the practice environment. In order to generate a more explosive start, he would shorten the track or have me start downhill. To represent different opponents, he raised and lowered the height of the quintain's shield. He changed the length of my lance, the weight. He even tied my right arm to my body, so I had to joust left-handed. "Tournaments are messy and unpredictable," he'd say. "You never know what problems you'll have to solve."

Practice was a puzzle that challenged my mind as much as my body. Whenever I got frustrated with a new constraint, I embraced my role as a problem solver and explored new paths. Yet even after all this time training under his methods, Gowyn could still surprise me.

One morning I found him at the corral, watching the black courser run. The horse moved with such power it was a wonder the fence could hold him. I walked down the hill to join

Gowyn, but when I got close, the horse shrieked and stormed to the back of the corral.

"Shadow's not used to company," Gowyn said.

We watched the animal in silence. It moved with a proud, defiant spirit, as if he could smash through the fence if it wanted.

"He's a marvelous animal," I said. "How come I've never seen you ride him?"

"Because I don't want to crack my skull. Shadow is skittish around people, especially crowds. He's still wild and defiant. I never had the heart to train it out of him. I doubt I even could."

Gowyn turned to me. "You and Snowfoot work well together," he said.

"I've ridden him since I was a child."

"He's not your typical jousting horse."

"Snowfoot has more spirit in him than a horse twice his size."

"I'm sure you're right. You two make a good team. But could you joust as well on another horse?" Gowyn looked back at the corral.

"You want me to ride Shadow? He won't let me near him."

"Ride him for a few passes," Gowyn said. "See if you can still hit your target."

I looked at the corral. Shadow stared back at me with equal unease. I didn't like the idea of jousting on this wild horse, but I wasn't going to back down from Gowyn's challenge. I left Snowfoot to snack at the apple tree and walked to the corral. The horse snorted as Gowyn opened the gate.

"Easy, Shadow," Gowyn said. "Easy."

I inched toward the horse. Shadow stomped the dirt and swung his head threateningly. I reached out my hand. The horse screeched and reared up. I stumbled to the ground and scurried away from his kicking hooves.

"Shadow would have made a fine tournament horse if he wasn't so shy," Gowyn said.

"I don't know if shy is the word I'd use," I said, dusting myself off.

"He spooks easily," Gowyn said. "He prefers to run in the dark."

"I've noticed." The rhythm of his stomping hooves kept me up at night.

Shadow put up a fight, but Gowyn was able to soothe him. He saddled the horse and led him out of the corral. He held Shadow still, whispering in his ear while I climbed on. The horse was bigger than Snowfoot, and it felt strange to be so high off the ground.

Snowfoot snorted from the shade of the apple tree as I took Shadow for a ride around the track. It took me a few minutes to get used to the rhythm of his powerful strides. Then I almost broke the reins getting him to stop.

"Looks like he's enjoying the exercise," Gowyn said.

"He wants to run," I said, trying to stay balanced.

"This is his chance." Gowyn handed me my practice lance.

I held Shadow's reins in one hand and raised my lance with the other. I'd hardly said "Yah" when Shadow took off, throwing me to the back of the saddle. I squeezed my legs against the horse's body, trying to stay upright as he tore down the track. By the time I regained my balance, we were twenty yards past the quintain.

"Whoa," I yelled and pulled the reins. Shadow came to a stop, snapping at the bit in his mouth.

Gowyn watched me from the other end of the track, waiting.

I turned Shadow around. "Let's try this again," I said.

Shadow sprung forward with a burst of speed. I lowered my lance to make a hurried strike, but Shadow veered away from the quintain at the last moment, and I never got the chance.

I pulled Shadow to a stop and bent close to his head.

"Listen," I said. "It's just me and Gowyn here. There's nothing to be afraid of. We're not stopping until we hit the target, so you can obey me and get this over with, or we can keep at it all day."

Shadow stomped a hoof in response.

"Ride straight this time." I looked down the track at the quintain's shield. "Yah!"

Shadow shot out like an arrow, but this time, I was ready. I caught my balance and leaned forward. We were speeding so fast we were almost at the quintain. There was no time for technique, only instinct. I thrust the lance at the quickly approaching target. My lance struck true. The tip struck the target so hard the shield split in two. The quintain was still spinning behind me as I wrestled Shadow to a stop.

Gowyn's face, usually calm, was full of surprise. "That blow would have unhorsed any knight."

"We were moving so fast," I said. "I don't know how I hit the target."

"You didn't have time to think, so you trusted."

I looked at the broken shield. The horse was fast, a true jousting horse. I flinched at the thought of an armored knight charging at me on the back of one of these powerful animals. A blow at this speed could be deadly.

"Let's go again," Gowyn said. "This time with Snowfoot."

I climbed off Shadow. The horse bucked as I hit the ground, and shot up the hill, happy to be free. "You and I both," I called after him.

After Shadow, riding Snowfoot was like walking. I shifted in rhythm with his smooth gait, knowing every move before it happened. I struck the target clean on the first try.

"Good boy," I said, petting Snowfoot's head. He snorted, as if jealous I would dare ride another horse.

"How did that pass feel?" Gowyn asked me.

"Effortless," I said. "Compared to Shadow, it felt like I was moving in slow motion."

Gowyn nodded. "You and Snowfoot have a clear bond. But that connection can lead to complacency. It's important to stretch yourself, to adapt to different situations. Like a new horse."

"That horse is crazy."

"Shadow is spirited. He can do amazing things when he's in control of himself, but he lets his temper get the better of him. Not unlike someone else I know."

"Something tells me there's a lesson here."

Gowyn smiled. "You are at your best when you let go of your need to prove yourself, Meridian. Your spirit makes you a fierce competitor. But you joust your best when you channel that spirit into calm, focused energy."

The ground thundered as Shadow raced past us.

Gowyn smiled. "Looks like Shadow is ready for another pass. You catch him this time. I have another shield to build."

I sighed and hurried after the wild black shape tearing across Gowyn's land. This was going to be a long day.

My Father's Armor

Fog blanketed the land as I walked down the path to the practice grounds. I waited beneath the apple tree with Snowfoot, eager to start. Training had been going well, and after three weeks working with Gowyn, I started to believe I might actually have a chance at the Tournament of Champions.

After a few minutes, Gowyn emerged from the fog, pushing a wheelbarrow. "Are you ready to try something new today?" he asked.

I almost laughed. With Gowyn, every day was something new. Practice was never pretty or comfortable. As he would say, "Do you want to feel good or do you want to get better?"

Gowyn stopped at the bottom of the path. "You've come a long way, Meridian. You should be proud of your hard work and your dedication to learning. I think it's time you took the next step in preparing for the tournament."

I approached the wheelbarrow. Inside were the two travel sacks I'd carried from home.

"What are we doing with my father's armor?" I asked.

"Remember our first lesson?"

"Practice for competition," I said. "But that's tournament armor. It's worth a fortune."

"Then it better work." Gowyn overturned a sack. The shining armor spilled out, clanging in the wheelbarrow.

I slowly put on my father's armor, trying not to get it dirty. With the muscle I'd put on, it almost fit. Gowyn helped me, showing me how to cinch on the various pieces. The process took forever, and when it was done, I could barely walk.

"How does anyone move in this stuff, let alone joust?"

"Better to find out now than on the day of the tournament," Gowyn said.

I tapped my breastplate with a gauntleted hand. "Can Snowfoot even carry me?"

"Another thing that's better discovered here."

One piece of armor remained in the wheelbarrow. I picked up my father's helmet. It was almost as if my father were staring at me through the flat eye-slit of the visor. I remembered him jousting in the armor; I'd watched from the stands, secretly dreaming that one day I'd compete under the banner of House Kay. Now, I wore the armor. And I felt its full weight.

I lowered the helmet over my head. It fit loosely, and I had to shift it until I could see out of the eye-slits.

"Are you ready?" Gowyn asked.

"Ready," my voice echoed back to me.

Snowfoot grunted under the weight but held still. Gowyn handed me the lance; it felt strange holding it with gauntlets. I shifted uncomfortably in the saddle. All freedom of movement was gone; I was trapped in a metal cage. But if I meant to compete in the tournament, then I had to get used to jousting in armor.

"Yah!" my voice echoed. But as soon as Snowfoot took off, the helmet twisted, blinding me. I clung to Snowfoot's neck and tried to rotate the visor back into place. The ground blurred by through the narrow line of vision. Snowfoot pulled to a stop at the end of the track before I'd even seen the target.

I tore off the helmet. "I can't see anything in this."

Gowyn walked up to the house and returned with a towel. "Try this."

He wrapped the thin cloth around my head. I put the helmet back on, positioning the eye-slit as best I could.

"I have some books in the house," he said. "Perhaps we could fill that head of yours before the tournament."

"Very funny."

He handed me my lance, and I rode Snowfoot to the start of the pass. The helmet still jostled, but at least I could see. I drew a line in my mind and waited behind it, on my thinking ground, until complaints of my armor faded. Then, focusing on my target, I crossed the line onto the trusting ground.

"Yah!" I called, and Snowfoot took off in a canter, cutting through the fog. I lost vision of my target but was able to regain it at the last moment. I struck the edge of the shield as I passed.

"You hit your target," Gowyn said, after I'd pulled Snowfoot to a stop.

"I grazed it."

"That's an improvement."

I huffed and adjusted my helmet. "I'm going again."

I rode a series of passes, only hitting the shield about a quarter of the time, and rarely true or with power. When I was ready to break the lance over my knee, Gowyn suggested I take a break.

"Learning is not a straight line," he said. "It'll take practice to get used to the armor. But you can learn it like any other skill."

But I had no time to waste; the Tournament of Champions was coming up quickly. I had to be ready. I yanked Snowfoot's reins with my heavy gauntlets. "Come on, boy."

I pushed into the afternoon, struggling through pass after pass. My jousting only grew worse. The more I rode, the angrier I became, and the less I hit my target. With the armor on, it was as if all the gains I'd made had been stripped away. Challenges that were once easy now seemed impossible. Suddenly, my chance of winning the tournament had vanished, and with it, any hope of repaying my family's debts.

After yet another failed attempt, I climbed down from Snowfoot and stormed toward the quintain. I let out a furious scream and smashed my lance against the shield. The quintain spun, and the sandbag struck me from behind. I hit the ground in a crash of metal. Air spilled from my lungs. I was buried under the weight of my father's armor. I stared up at the grey sky through the slit in my visor, tears clouding my vision.

Then Gowyn was there, helping me to my feet. When I could stand, I tore off my helmet and began shedding the armor.

"It's no use," I said, my voice breaking. I threw pieces of armor across the practice grounds, the once shining metal now tarnished in dirt.

"Meridian."

"I can't do it." I turned, unable to meet Gowyn's eyes. I'd failed, and that stung worse than any pain.

"Meridian, it'll take time. You can't expect—"

I ran before he could finish. I fled the practice grounds and disappeared up the hill into the grey fog where the mist would hide my tears. My legs burned, my heart pounded in my chest, but I kept running, taking the pain.

How blind I'd been. I had no business competing in the Tournament of Champions. I was too weak. All the training, the dreaming, it had been a waste, a child's fantasy. My mother had been right all along: I was a fool to believe I could be more than who I was.

A Knight's Oath

I wandered through the fog for hours. I was ashamed of my outburst, yet there was another feeling as well: one of relief. The weight of my impossible goal had been lifted. I no longer had to fight fate and carve my own path. I didn't have to be a knight.

Rounding a hill, I stumbled upon a splash of color in the grey. Two flower beds lay side by side. I stopped to admire the vibrant arrangements, wondering why Gowyn kept them so far from his house. Then I saw the headstones.

I gasped and stepped back. As I stared at the two graves, the world reshaped before me. Up to that point, I'd only thought of Gowyn as my teacher; I knew nothing of the man. Even the legendary Grey Knight must have had a family. Was this why he'd stopped jousting and disappeared from tournaments?

Staring at the graves, I wondered where my father was buried. Perhaps in the shade of the great oak beside the practice grounds. It hurt to think that I may never see his resting place.

. . .

I returned to find Gowyn on his knees in the garden. I walked to the garden's edge and apologized for my temper and for running away. But I told him he couldn't talk me out of quitting. My mind was made up.

Gowyn nodded and continued digging up carrots. "I understand."

"I'm done with the tournament, and I'm done with jousting."

Gowyn didn't look up.

"I'm wasting my time and yours. I'll never be good enough to compete against real knights."

Gowyn wiped the dirt from a carrot and placed it in the basket. "There's nothing wrong with being afraid, Meridian. It's natural to feel pressure. You've taken on a tremendous challenge."

"What's the point of all this training? Of battering myself to exhaustion every day? I have no chance of winning."

"Is winning the only reason to compete?"

"It's the only way I'm going to save my family's land."

Gowyn looked at me curiously. "Why jousting?"

"What?"

"There are easier ways to earn money than to become the world's best jouster."

"I thought I was good at it," I said. "But I was a fool to think I could become a knight."

Gowyn sat up and rested his hands on his hips.

"Did you know I almost quit after my first major tournament?"

"You did?"

Gowyn nodded. "I was not yet twenty. I was bigger than other boys my age, and I'd won every local tournament I entered. That early success nearly ruined me."

"How?"

"Confident in my skills, I traveled to Warwick to compete against a field of English champions. I was unhorsed in the second round. Nearly split my skull. I don't know what stung more, the pain to my body or my pride. I thought I was special, destined for greatness, and a lance humbled me in an instant. If I'd have found a willing buyer, I'd have sold my horse and armor that very night."

"What did you do?" I asked. "What made you continue?"

The hint of a grin formed on the edge of Gowyn's lips. "I remembered the reason I'd started jousting. Because I loved it. I loved pushing myself beyond what I thought possible, to be the best I could be. Losing hadn't proven that I was unworthy. It taught me what I needed to work on. I swallowed my pride and returned to the tournament the next day and watched. I studied every knight, for I knew I'd face them again. And the next time, I'd be better."

Gowyn looked at me with a piercing stare.

"I'm not going to motivate you, Meridian. Jousting is a harsh sport. I've seen it break the strongest men. But if you do continue, know this: Every knight gets hit; every knight falls. But champions refuse to stay down."

I turned and looked at the quintain and the churned up practice grounds. I thought back to the long summer days of training with my father. How I'd beg him for one more pass, even after the sun went down and it was too dark to see. All I'd ever wanted to do was joust. When had it become a burden?

"Gowyn," I said. "Have you always lived here alone?"

Gowyn stared at the basket of carrots for a long time. I feared I'd crossed a line until he finally spoke. "No. Not always." He looked up and took a deep breath. "I had a wife. And a daughter. They died some time ago."

"I don't mean to pry. If you don't want to talk about it . . ."

Gowyn looked into the distance. Toward the graves.

"I spent my life away from them," he said. "When I wasn't off fighting in the war, I competed in tournaments. I was good at it. I won events all over England. I gained fame and fortune and was honored by the king himself. It felt good to stand victorious over others, to hear crowds chant my name. I thought it brought me honor as a knight."

Gowyn's hand dug into the ground, gathering a handful of dirt.

"I was to leave for a tournament in France when my daughter fell ill. I'd been summoned by the king to represent England. My wife begged me to stay, but I told her I was an honorable knight. I had a duty to my king.

"I won the tournament and returned home to find my wife and child dead. Had I been here . . . perhaps I could have done something. If only to hold my daughter as she passed. Instead, I was gone, seeking glory."

Gowyn loosened his grip, letting the dirt slide through his fist.

"The day I buried them, I put away my lance and armor, and I swore an oath that I would never leave my family again. And a knight's oath is sacred."

We waited in silence for a moment and then I asked, "Do you ever wonder if your life would have been better if you never became a knight?"

"I think about it often," he said. "I think of all the choices I made and all the different paths I could have taken."

"Do you wish you had quit jousting after that first loss?"

Gowyn stood up and wiped his hands on his pants. "I've suffered many losses, Meridian. And I've failed at many things. But that I got up after that loss and continued to fight has brought me more honor than any trophy can."

Gowyn went up to the house, and I remained behind. I walked the practice grounds, thinking of my own story and how hard life had been since I'd chosen this path. It would be so much easier to run home and fulfill my obligations as a noble lady. No more falls, no more bruises. No more training until I couldn't stand. No more risking failure.

There came a familiar snort. I turned to find Snowfoot standing under the apple tree. His deep black eyes watched me. I threw my arms around his neck. Snowfoot stood still while I clung to him. I felt the same comfort in his presence I'd felt since the day I picked him.

The fog had begun to lift. Color returned to the farm. Above me, the branches were weighed down by apples. The once-green fruit now had a red hue.

I sighed and ran a hand through Snowfoot's mane. "What are we going to do?"

Snowfoot remained still, waiting for my lead. In my heart, I knew I couldn't go home yet. I couldn't live the rest of my days, never knowing how good I could have been. I pressed my head against Snowfoot's. "If I do this, are you with me, boy?"

Snowfoot nudged me and sniffed at my hair. I bent down and picked up my father's helmet, wiping away the dirt.

"I may not be a knight," I said. "But I can live as one."

There, in the shade of the apple tree, I swore an oath. I swore to give everything I had to my training and to surrender the outcome. If I lost at the Tournament of Champions, it would be because I wasn't good enough. It wouldn't be because I quit.

Mindfulness

From then on, I never practiced jousting unless I was in full armor. We worked through our previous challenges, starting with hitting the target at speed and then adding a moving target and changing the environment. It was frustrating going backward, and a part of me wanted to quit, but each time I remembered my oath and pressed on. I took my share of falls, but I never stayed down. After a week of hard training, I was catching up to where I'd been without the burden of armor.

It was late afternoon. We sat on the porch, having finished our daily practice reflection. "You're showing remarkable improvement," Gowyn said afterward. "And you look more comfortable in your armor."

I shook my head. "I think I'm just getting used to being uncomfortable." I sat silently, watching Shadow eat from his trough.

"What's on your mind, Meridian?" Gowyn asked.

"The tournament," I said with a sigh. "I know I'm getting better, but I still feel so nervous."

"It helps to be mindful of your feelings."

"What does mindful mean?"

"Mindfulness is being fully present, aware of what you're doing, thinking, sensing, or feeling in the moment. And presence is the key to performance."

"I don't understand. How does being present help you joust?"

"A joust is won or lost in the blink of an eye. You can't perform your best when your head is somewhere else."

I was reminded of my father's words: *Keep your head and your feet in the same place.* He'd talked about how a knight had to be mentally strong, but he never explained how to develop that strength. Did Gowyn know?

"How does mindfulness help?" I asked. "Will it stop nerves and negative thoughts?"

Gowyn shook his head. "Think of your attention like a boat, and your mind is the ocean. The ocean is always producing waves in the form of thoughts and feelings. Sometimes the waves are gentle. Sometimes they become a storm and crash into the boat. You can't stop the waves, but you can set an anchor so they don't knock you too far off course. That is the practice of mindfulness, and you can strengthen it like any other skill."

"How do I practice?"

"By being aware of the thoughts and feelings you're experiencing, without judgment. Simply note them and let them pass."

"What if they don't pass?"

"Let's try an exercise." Gowyn sat up straight and rested his hands in his lap. "Close your eyes."

I followed his example and closed my eyes.

"Now, listen to the waves. When you feel a thought or feeling, note it aloud. There is no wrong answer. There is no judgement. Simply acknowledge what you feel in the present moment."

I sighed, stirring uncomfortably in the silence. I felt foolish sitting there with my eyes closed. What was I supposed to say?

Then came Gowyn's calm voice. "There is anticipation."

Gowyn continued noting his feelings aloud in a detached voice. There was a pause between each, like waves receding. "There is patience . . . There is concern."

My pulse quickened. I didn't feel comfortable opening up. I would rather get hit with the sandbag than share my feelings. I thought about quitting the exercise and then remembered my oath. If this could make me a better jouster, I'd give it a try.

My first impulse was to make up something, to say what a brave knight should feel. Instead, I admitted what I really felt: "There is discomfort."

Gowyn exhaled. "There is understanding."

I took a deep breath and listened to my mind, noting feelings as they came: "There is impatience . . . There is nervousness . . . There is calm."

After a few minutes of noting, I opened my eyes and met Gowyn's gaze.

"What did you notice?" he asked.

"When I stopped worrying about what I should be feeling, it was easier to identify what I was feeling."

Gowyn nodded. "It's easier to hear with a quiet mind. What else did you notice?"

I thought back to the exercise, to the words I chose. "The feelings changed."

"What does that tell you?"

"That the feelings come and go. Like waves."

Gowyn nodded. "A feeling is temporary. You may feel nervous or confident in one moment, but that feeling passes. It doesn't control your actions."

"But shouldn't a knight be confident all the time?"

Gowyn rubbed his beard. "When I was younger, there was a

knight in our realm who was renowned for his jousting. He was bigger and stronger than the other knights. His horse was faster. He went from town to town and never lost a duel. People believed he was unbeatable, himself most of all.

"In one town, his challenge was accepted by a boy who'd just been knighted. Facing off against the fledgling knight, the champion had all the confidence in the world."

"But he didn't win, did he?" I said.

Gowyn shook his head. "The boy unhorsed him on the first pass."

I smiled. Though it wasn't my story, it made me feel that I too could overcome impossible odds.

"What do you think the champion's feeling of confidence did for him?" Gowyn asked.

"It hurt him because he underestimated his opponent."

"Now consider the boy. This was his first tournament. He was competing against a champion knight. He had no reason to be confident, yet he still won."

"So, you don't need confidence to win."

"Feelings affect us because we're human, but they don't control us. We choose who we want to be."

Gowyn turned and fixed his eyes on me.

"Feelings are fleeting, Meridian. Trust in your training. Trust in your process. Then ride. That's all a knight can do."

"The boy in the story," I said. "That was you, wasn't it?"

Gowyn smiled. "Yes."

"Were you nervous?"

Gowyn chuckled. "I was a mess. I threw up my breakfast in the stables before I rode out. Barely got my helmet off in time."

We both laughed, and I felt some of my unease slip away.

"No matter how many tournaments I won, I felt nervous before every duel," Gowyn said.

"You did?"

"It's natural to be nervous when the outcome is uncertain. To feel pressure simply means you care, that you're doing something important."

I smiled, feeling a rush of relief. The doubts I had were normal, and they didn't control me.

I sat on Gowyn's porch, feeling my chest rise and fall with every breath. Since I'd left home, hardly a moment went by when I didn't think about the tournament. But right now, I didn't want to look past this moment. I wanted my head right where my feet were.

"Thank you, Gowyn," I said. "I'm grateful to have you as my teacher."

Gowyn raised an eyebrow. "There is vulnerability. We must be making progress." We both laughed. "How would you feel about continuing the exercise?"

In answer, I closed my eyes and listened, mindful of what feeling came.

"There is excitement," I said.

The Gift

Light shined through the cracks in the barn. I covered my head with the pillow, longing for the soft sheets of my old bed and a set of heavy curtains. After so many weeks of training, I wanted to stay in bed and skip practice. I took a moment to note the feelings of fatigue and soreness. Then I reminded myself why I was doing this. I pulled the pillow away and got ready for practice.

The ground chilled my bare feet as I climbed out of bed and stretched my stiff body. Riding Shadow in full armor had produced soreness in muscles I'd never felt before. I hoped whatever surprise Gowyn had in store for me today didn't involve that demon horse.

I stepped out of the barn, surprised by the brightness. The sun was already poking over the mountains! I quickly saddled Snowfoot and hurried down the path to start the day's training. I stopped when I reached the apple tree, looking around in confusion. The quintain was gone. How was I going to practice?

A rope held up by stakes now stretched along the track, marking a barrier like a real tournament. Moving closer to the track, I discovered a pile of lances. Unlike my sturdy practice lance, these lances were made of ash. Their tips were crown-shaped with three blunt metal prongs. These were real tournament lances. I picked one up, getting used to the length and weight.

Heavy footsteps sounded behind me. I turned and gasped at the sight of the massive knight descending the path. Rust stained his armor. A soaring eagle adorned his helmet.

"Gowyn?"

The imposing figure of the Grey Knight stopped before me. He lifted a creaky visor in salute. "It's tighter than I remember," Gowyn said. "But it'll have to do."

I stared at him. "What are you doing?"

"You've gone about as far as you can practicing against the quintain. You need to face a real opponent."

"I'm going to joust you?"

"We don't have much choice." He lifted his arms. The metal creaked. "Luckily, I never got around to throwing this away."

I stared at the armored figure with the eagle emblem. I couldn't believe it; I was going to joust the Grey Knight.

"Well, don't just stand there," Gowyn said. "Help me wrangle Shadow."

It took both of us to coerce the horse out of the corral. The mighty courser who ran so gracefully under cover of night was wild and unruly in the daylight. I held his reins as Gowyn mounted. The horse bucked and almost sent Gowyn to the ground.

"Easy, boy," Gowyn said, petting Shadow's black mane. "Easy. It's just us."

With the horse settled down, Gowyn turned his attention to me. "It's time to prepare for competition. Practice your routine as if this were the tournament. Start on your thinking ground and don't cross to the trusting ground until you're ready."

I drew a lance and climbed onto Snowfoot, eager for a real joust. I looked down the track at Gowyn with the legendary eagle's emblem on his helmet. The imaginary battles of my childhood had come true: I was dueling the Grey Knight. I took a deep breath and focused on my mission. Then I raised my lance and crossed onto the trusting ground.

I quickly saw how different it was training against a live opponent. It took time for Snowfoot to get comfortable riding with Shadow charging at him. Gowyn tried his best to rein the horse in, but Shadow was unpredictable and as likely to hit the rope barrier as stay to the right-hand side.

With a moving opponent, the timing of my passes changed. I had to lower my lance and lock it into place sooner. Visually, there was so much to take in. Each of Gowyn's movements mattered. They showed his intention and numerous possible threats I had to counteract at lightning speed. Each pass was a new puzzle to solve. Fortunately, I had practiced facing the unexpected. I let go of worry and stayed present.

I trusted.

Despite not jousting in decades, Gowyn proved a formidable opponent. And with Shadow's speed, wild as it was, he was nearly impossible to hit cleanly. Over the course of my training, I'd developed expert aim, but I hadn't faced a lance striking at me. Even the passes where Gowyn didn't strike, allowing me to work on some new skill, my body tightened in panic. And when he did strike, his lance was like a battering ram. I took hit after hit but kept going. This is what I had longed for. This was "practicing on the high board."

I was so focused on every pass, losing myself in the thrill of jousting Gowyn, I didn't notice the sun had set. We broke for the day and corralled Shadow.

"Jousting is a lot harder when there's someone riding against you," I said.

Gowyn removed his helmet. His face was red, and his grey hair was matted to his forehead. "That's the gift of an opponent."

"What do you mean?"

"It's easy to look at our opponents as enemies. But without them, there is no tournament. Without them, you'll never be pushed to be your best. Like any challenge, a worthy opponent is a gift." Gowyn cracked his neck with a grunt. "What gift did you find?"

I thought through our training and what facing a real opponent had taught me. "I see now I need to get better at defending myself."

Gowyn nodded. "Always be learning, Meridian. In victory and defeat."

He tried to take a step and grimaced, catching himself on my shoulder. "Now, help me up to the house."

As I helped Gowyn's worn-out body up the hill, I realized just how much he was sacrificing to train me. The old knight had given up tournaments, hadn't touched a lance in decades, yet he had donned his armor once again for me. I felt a rush of appreciation as we walked the path together. He was giving me a gift, and I would do everything I could to honor it.

Blue Sky

As the weeks went on, Gowyn pushed practice to later in the morning so I could recover from the intensity of our training. I'd learned a lot practicing against the quintain, but while the contraption had honed my power and aim, only a real opponent could prepare me for a duel. I needed experience jousting against a live lance. Experience, Gowyn provided. Not even the quintain's sandbag had prepared me for the sting of his blows.

He pushed me on every pass, always staying slightly ahead of me. The better I got, the harder he went. He rode at me with different styles, attacking at different angles, trying to catch me off guard. But I was a quick learner and never fell for the same move twice.

With the tournament now only weeks away, I'd been incorporating the trusting mindset more and more in practice. Though I still fell back to overthinking and judgment, there were times I rode free. It was on those passes that I was at my best.

We finished practice for the day, and I helped Gowyn off of

Shadow and out of his armor. It was clear the price his body was paying to joust against me, but he never complained. He just moved slower and was not quick to get up from meals or our afternoon reflections. Perhaps the added morning's rest wasn't just for my benefit after all.

"You've improved a lot since you stumbled out of the forest, Meridian Kay," Gowyn said. "It's impressive how much you've grown."

"I hope it'll be enough," I said, wiping sweat from my brow.

Instead of reflecting on the day's practice as we normally did, Gowyn told me to follow him. We walked from the torn up track to the green hills on the backside of his farm. The sun, arcing toward the trees, was still warm on my skin.

"Are you worried about the tournament?" Gowyn asked.

There were only a couple weeks left before the Tournament of Champions, and I could think of little else. What once was a distant goal now rumbled like a storm on the horizon. In a short time, my days of training on Gowyn's farm would be over, and I would face the best knights in the world. As a little girl, I'd dreamed of that day. Now, I felt both excitement and dread.

"I love jousting," I said. "My whole life I've wanted to be a champion knight. But now that I finally have the chance to compete, it feels like too much. I wish I could just keep training here on your farm."

"Pressure is a privilege," Gowyn said. "It tests us, and it can bring out the best in us."

He stopped on the side of a hill and motioned me to sit on the grass. I prepared for another mindfulness exercise, which had become part of our daily practice routine, but Gowyn did not join me.

"Try something," he said. "Close your eyes. Picture yourself at the tournament. You are atop Snowfoot on the tournament field, hidden in your armor, jousting before the king and a throng of spectators."

I winced. Imagining the King of England and a crowd of hostile foreigners watching me made my gut tighten.

"What could go wrong?" Gowyn asked.

"I can think of a hundred things," I said.

"Name them."

I sighed, thinking through the various fears that kept me awake at night.

"I could lose. I could embarrass myself in front of thousands of people. I could dishonor my father's name. I could be discovered as a girl and be imprisoned for posing as a knight. I could be injured, maimed, or killed."

I opened my eyes. Gowyn looked at me with compassion. "That's a lot to worry about."

"Huh. I thought you were going to tell me not to worry, and that everything will be fine."

"There's nothing wrong with what you feel, Meridian. This is a hard thing you're taking on. It's natural to be scared."

"That doesn't make me feel any better."

"What about in your head?" Gowyn asked. "What thoughts might come up that would stop you from being your best?"

There were so many outside forces to worry about, I hadn't even thought how my mind would try to sabotage me.

"Distractions," I said, remembering our mindfulness lessons. "Thinking about the crowd or my mistakes or anything that takes my focus away from jousting."

Gowyn nodded. "Attention drives performance. Worrying about things outside of your three-foot world could pull you out of the present. What else?"

I frowned. "I've never competed in a tournament before. And this is the Tournament of Champions. Maybe I'm not good enough? Maybe I don't belong there?"

Gowyn nodded again. "Those thoughts may come up."

"Is this supposed to help me?" I asked. "Focusing on everything that could go wrong?"

Gowyn sat next to me on the hill. "It's preparing," he said. "Like trying on your armor, it is better to face the obstacles now than to be surprised by them in the tournament. It's better to have a plan."

"Try this exercise," Gowyn continued. "Take the thought, 'I don't belong here.' Live with it for a moment. Feel what it does to you."

I closed my eyes and repeated the doubt that had so often plagued me: *I don't belong here. I don't belong here.* An image appeared in my head. I was at the tournament, holding my helmet in shaking hands, tears streaking down my face. The other knights, the crowd, everyone saw me for the fraud I was.

"Now," Gowyn said. "Try this: 'I'm having the thought I don't belong here. I'm having the thought I don't belong here.'"

I closed my eyes and repeated the new phrase. *I'm having the thought I don't belong here. I'm having the thought I don't belong here.*

"You've lived with those two thoughts," Gowyn said after a moment. "Now, try this one: 'I notice I'm having the thought I don't belong here. I notice I'm having the thought I don't belong here.'"

I notice I'm having the thought I don't belong here. I notice I'm having the thought I don't belong here.

After a moment of repeating the thought, I opened my eyes.

"Was there a difference in how the three thoughts made you feel?" Gowyn asked.

"The first one hurt," I said, remembering the pain of the phrase. "But the others didn't have the same sting. With the third, I felt detached from the feeling."

Gowyn nodded. "You are facing a great challenge, Meridian. Negative thoughts will come up. You can choose to believe them and let them control you, or you can notice them for what they are: just thoughts. You choose how you will act. You decide what kind of person you're going to be."

I thought about the negative thoughts swirling inside my head. As powerful as they felt at times, they didn't need to control my actions. A voice may tell me I'm not good enough to joust. But, I could choose courage and ride anyway.

"What if the worries and doubts are too much?" I asked. "How can I cross to the trusting ground if my trust is gone?"

"Think of yourself at your best," Gowyn said. "When you are completely focused and present and the target comes to you. Now imagine that best self as a bright blue sky. That blue sky is always there, always above you. But thoughts, emotions, judgment, fear, doubt, negative talk can appear like clouds, hiding the blue sky. In our darkest moments, we look up and all we see is a storm."

"How do I find the blue sky again?" I asked. "Do I just ignore the clouds?"

"Be mindful of the negative thoughts and recognize them for what they are: information. If doubt comes, note it and use the information. 'There is doubt. When there is doubt, I might grow timid. So, I'll choose to be more aggressive on this next pass.' See the clouds and then let them blow away by focusing on who you want to be: the blue sky. Recognize, release, refocus."

"Recognize, release, refocus," I said.

"When you release thoughts and distractions and focus on your mission, you can tap into your best self. That is the trusting mindset."

I looked up at the late blue sky peeking through the clouds. I imagined each of those clouds as a separate negative thought: a doubt about my ability, a fear of not knowing enough, of not being strong enough, of letting my father down. One by one, the clouds passed, giving way to patches of blue.

"Remember, the blue sky is always there," Gowyn said. "Even when you can't see it."

The Inner Knight

I rode down the right side of the track. Ahead of me, Gowyn opened to attack, his breastplate in full view. I had a clear shot and took it, throwing all my weight into the strike. But as I drove my lance forward, Gowyn did the unexpected. He leaned back. My lance passed over him, narrowly missing his helmet. He stuck his lance out sideways. It was like riding full speed into a tree branch. The lance slapped against the top of my breastplate. My head whipped back, and I tumbled off Snowfoot, landing in a clang of armor.

It took me a few moments to catch my breath. Dazed, I climbed to a knee and removed my helmet.

"That was a dirty shot," I said.

"Was it?" Gowyn dismounted Shadow; the black horse helped him with a wild buck. "I hit you with my lance." Gowyn took my hand and helped me to my feet.

"That's not how you joust."

"You're seeing only one path again. Remember, you're a problem solver. Many roads can take you where you want to go, if you're open to them."

I shook my head. "I guess I'm just not creative."

"Is that right? And were you born a good jouster?"

"No," I said, remembering our talk about the first time I jousted. I knew where this was going.

"And how did you get better?"

"I practiced. I focused on being better tomorrow than I was today."

Gowyn nodded. "Creativity is a skill and can be developed like any other. Be careful of the story you tell yourself. Our beliefs matter. You can learn. You can grow. You can do hard things."

"I can learn. I can grow. I can do hard things."

Gowyn smiled. "I believe you."

We marched up the path to the house and began our daily reflection. I analyzed practice, telling Gowyn what I did well—hunting the good stuff—and areas I could improve. The reflections had become so routine, I no longer took it personally. We talked about my performance as if it were separate from me. I wasn't less of a person because I missed a read or exposed my body too early. It was simply information. A practice that exposed a weakness was a gift. For that weakness was no longer hidden; it was something I could work on.

By the time we finished our reflection, the sun had sunk behind the forest.

"I can't believe my time here is coming to an end," I said. "I feel like a different person than the girl that came here. I don't know if my family would even recognize me."

"I think they'd be proud of you," Gowyn said.

I smiled and met Gowyn's eyes, no longer finding it uncomfortable to hold his gaze. "I know I'll never be a real knight. But I wanted to thank you for making me feel like one for the past couple months. It's what I always dreamed of."

Gowyn's face turned suddenly serious. "A title does not make one honorable, Meridian. We are measured by our character. You have shown the traits of a knight: dedication, courage, compassion. Continue to follow your inner knight, and you will live a life of honor."

"My inner knight?"

"There is a voice inside you that speaks with fear, keeping you safe from danger and risk. This is the voice most people hear. But there is a second voice. One that tells you not to run, but to take up your lance and ride toward that danger. This is the voice of your inner knight. When you are tested, when you face battles and moments of darkness, you can listen to fear, or you can embrace your inner knight."

Gowyn leaned back, stretching his sore back. "Let's do another exercise. It has to do with the stories we tell ourselves."

"All right," I said.

"Who is someone you admire?"

I thought for a moment. An image appeared in my head, a happy memory. "My father."

"What is it you admire about him?"

"He wasn't afraid to pursue his dreams. I see now how he must have struggled and doubted himself after losing. But he kept showing up to the practice grounds. He kept working and pushing himself to be a champion, yet he also prized staying in the moment."

"It sounds like he was brave, present, and resilient."

"He was."

"And those values are important to you as well."

"Yes. I want to be champion."

"Winning the tournament is a goal. A value is different from a goal. A value is your heart's desire for how you want to behave. A goal is a destination, it is achieved, or it isn't. But values are the directions you take. They have no ending. They must be lived every day. When we're clear on our values, we know what we stand for and who we want to be. We know how to act in the face of obstacles and negative emotions."

I thought of the obstacles that stood before me. I couldn't control how I finished in the Tournament of Champions, but I could control how I competed. No matter what happened, I could live out my values.

"I want to be brave, present, and resilient like my father," I said.

"What will it look like to live out those values in the tournament?"

"I won't back down from a challenge, even if I'm afraid. I'll focus on one pass at a time. And if I get hit, I won't stay down. I'll listen to my inner knight."

"That sounds like a powerful story to me," Gowyn said.

As I lay in bed, I thought of my inner knight, imagining shining armor just below the surface of my skin, and a brave voice speaking up during moments of fear. I may not carry the same title as my opponents at the Tournament of Champions, but I could still compete with the courage of a true knight.

Farewell

By the last weeks of training, all the skills I'd developed—mental and physical—were coming together. I'd caught up to Gowyn. His experience no longer outweighed my speed and accuracy. When we dueled at full force, I got the better of him more times than not. On the final day before the tournament, I was jousting better than ever. My excitement to compete overshadowed my nerves. I was ready to test myself against the best jousters in the world.

But the tournament could wait until tomorrow. I still had work to do.

I held Snowfoot on the thinking ground as I went through my routine, releasing distracting thoughts with my breath. Then I crossed onto the trusting ground with one focus: "Powerful."

"Yah!" Snowfoot flew down the track. Gowyn and Shadow charged straight for us, lance drawn back to strike. I didn't back down. I lowered my head against the coming blow and thrust with all my power. My lance shattered to splinters against Gowyn's breastplate. I pulled Snowfoot to a stop and turned to see Gowyn slumped in the saddle. I jumped down and raced to his side.

"Gowyn, are you all right?"

"Now that was a hit," Gowyn groaned. He removed his helmet and grimaced. "Maybe I shouldn't have taught you to dent armor."

We dismounted and broke down our equipment. Free of his saddle, Shadow sprinted off across the green hills. I watched him run, unable to believe my training with Gowyn had come to an end. Snowfoot rested in the shade. I joined him, picking a bright red apple from the tree that had lured us there all those months ago.

"I can't believe the tournament starts tomorrow," I said. I bit into the apple. It was ripe and juicy. "Do you think I have any chance of winning?"

Gowyn rubbed his grey beard. "I think you've put in as much work as you could and prepared like a champion. Now it's time to trust yourself and let your skills out."

"Thank you for all you've done for me, Gowyn," I said. "I don't know what would have become of me if I hadn't met you."

"It has been an honor, Meridian. Though, I'm glad you'll finally have other opponents to pick on."

"I'm excited to see York and the tournament grounds. Where will we stay? Do you think knights are really coming from all over the world?"

Gowyn looked away. "Why don't you pack. I'll make dinner."

Without another word, Gowyn limped up the path to the house. I raced to the barn with Snowfoot and began packing. I opened the king's invitation for the hundredth time and traced my finger over the name "Sir Kay." Then I overturned a bucket and sat down to buff my father's armor. As I scrubbed the metal, I pictured myself jousting at the Tournament of Champions. My heart raced and nerves began to claw at my insides. But I remembered that nerves were natural. I took a deep breath and focused on my three-foot world. I didn't have to win the tournament right now. I just had to shine armor.

I entered Gowyn's house and found him at the table, staring at the plates of food. Our dinners were usually alive with talk of the day's practice or what stories I could pry from him. But now we ate in silence. Something was wrong.

"You haven't packed," I said, looking around the house.

Gowyn, who usually held my gaze with a confident stare, now avoided my eyes.

"We'll need to leave early," I said. "I have to find a way into the tournament. Otherwise, all of this work will have been for nothing."

"Is that what you think?"

"No, of course not. I wouldn't trade my time here for anything. I've learned so much. But I need to find out how good I can be."

Gowyn nodded. "I know you'll compete with honor, Meridian. I wish I could see it, but I can't go with you."

"What! What do you mean?" Panic seized me. Riding into York, posing as my father, battling in the Tournament of Champions—I didn't think I'd be facing these challenges alone!

"I'm sorry," Gowyn said. "But you don't need me. You're ready for this."

"I don't understand. What did I do wrong?"

"You did nothing wrong. You are an excellent student and a gifted jouster. But my place is here. With my family."

"After all our training, don't you care how I do?"

"I care about *you*, Meridian."

I jumped back. The chair clattered to the floor. "What about your own advice? You talk of being present, but you're the one living in the past."

"I swore an oath that I would never leave my family. A sacred oath I cannot break. My honor is all I have left."

"All you have left..."

I spun around and threw the door open.

"Meridian," Gowyn called as I ran down the porch steps into the night. "Meridian, wait."

But I didn't turn back. I ran to the barn and saddled Snowfoot. Then I lifted the sacks of my father's armor onto his back. I couldn't stay at Gowyn's farm for another minute. I threw on my travel cloak and climbed onto Snowfoot.

"It's just you and me, boy," I said. "As always."

We rode out of the barn, down the path from Gowyn's house.

"Meridian, wait!" he called after me.

I pushed Snowfoot into a gallop. He tore through the churned-up dirt that had served as my training ground. Gowyn's voice called again, but I didn't look back. Waves of anger raged in me; I couldn't see through the storm. In the darkness behind me, I heard a second set of hooves as Shadow raced around his corral.

We reached the main road and didn't slow until we were far from Gowyn's farm. I caught my breath, ashamed. After all my training, I'd let my emotions control me. I knew Gowyn had a reason not to leave, but I still felt abandoned. Pride prevented me from turning around.

"I don't need him," I told myself. "I don't need anyone."

Under the cloud of moonlight, I rode to York alone.

York

The city of York was like nothing I'd ever encountered. It announced itself with towering twin spires that could be seen from every direction. Its buildings were taller than great pines and as numerous as a forest. Shops and houses were pressed together, and an endless river of people flowed through the streets and narrow alleyways. The sound of so many in one place was deafening. Trash and rotten food lay in the muddy street, and I had to cover my nose as I walked Snowfoot past streams of wastewater.

I stopped before a shop and gazed at the fine clothes in the window. Two women emerged from the shop wearing dresses of the brightest fabric I'd ever seen. They stopped and stared at me in disgust. I suddenly realized what I must look like. I'd spent the night in a field just outside the city. My braid had come undone, and my hair must be as wild as beach grass. But more than that, I hadn't thought of my looks for the past months. My clothes were torn and dirty and hardly fit my now muscular body. I desperately needed a bath and new clothes, but I had no money. I ducked my head and moved on.

As we walked, the noisy, cramped streets opened up. In the

fields outside the city stood tents and large pavilions. Some camps were packed with spectators who'd come to watch the tournament. Others housed the competitors themselves. Flags and banners hung from the pavilions, displaying a knight's country and house. Crowds circled around men in armor who sparred or practiced with their squires.

Then I came upon the tournament grounds. I ran to the fence and gazed at an arena big enough to fit a village. Rope barriers marked the center of three jousting tracks. Viewing areas bordered the field, including a large, shaded pavilion for noble lords and ladies. By afternoon, the eyes of Europe would be on this field. What would they make of me?

I grasped the letter in my pocket. First, I would need to get in the tournament.

I walked around the tournament grounds, asking for directions. The first two men I encountered snorted at my accent and went about their business. The third, however, pointed me in the direction of the registration tent. I hurried across the grounds, thinking of what I would say. I tied Snowfoot within sight of the entrance and went inside. The competitors in line before me were a head taller and twice as wide. They wore fine garments and their hair was neatly combed. Even the squires looked like lords compared to me. I pawed at my hair, trying in vain to mat it into place. The looks on the faces of the noble knights told me I didn't belong. But I held my place, my eyes fixed on the back of the man ahead of me. I wasn't in York to attend a ball, after all. I'd come to joust.

When my turn arrived, I stepped forward, clutching the king's invitation. The steward was a round man whose heavy brow folded into a scowl as I approached the table. "Yes?"

I froze, my voice caught in my throat.

"The tournament field doesn't open until the afternoon," the steward snapped. "You can find a seat then."

"I'm here to enter the tournament," I said, finding my voice. "For Sir William Kay."

"Who?"

"Sir William Kay of Scotland."

"And who are you?"

"I . . . I'm his squire."

"A girl squire?" The steward scoffed. "And will Sir Kay be competing on a cow?"

This drew snickers from the men in the tent. I felt the eyes of the knights behind me. I didn't belong there and everyone knew it.

"This is the Tournament of Champions, not some farm festival." The steward waved a dismissive hand. "Begone."

"Sir William Kay is a champion," I said. "He is a great Scottish knight."

"Entry denied."

I held up the letter. "But I have an invitation—"

"Must I call the guards, girl?"

A man shoved me aside and approached the table. I stumbled back as if I'd been struck. After how far I'd come—the work I'd put in, the months of training—to be defeated before stepping foot on the tournament field . . . No. I'd sooner rot in an English cell than return home, never having taken my shot.

I pushed my way back to the front of the line and slammed the letter on the table. "I demand to see the king."

"What?" the steward exclaimed.

I pointed to the bottom of the invitation. "This is his signature, is it not? If the king intends to break his word, I'd like to hear it from his mouth, not some underling's."

The tent fell silent. The steward's face burned red. His chair toppled over as he rose, ready to explode. But before he could summon the guards, a chuckle filled the tent. A fierce-looking man with black hair and a dagger-shaped chin pushed through the knights to the steward's table. He wore a blood-red tunic, and the longsword on his belt nearly scraped the ground.

"The Scot's got some fire," the man said. He looked me over. "If the rest of her people had her heart, we'd still be at war."

"Sir Payne," the steward stammered. "I apologize. The girl was just leaving."

"I was not," I said. "Not before Sir Kay is registered for the tournament."

"Sir Kay?" The English knight turned to me. "I've never heard of him."

"Then you must not have competed in Scotland."

The corners of Sir Payne's lips rose in mild amusement, but the smile never reached his wolfish eyes.

"Did Sir Kay receive a summons?" he asked the steward.

The round man glanced at the letter with a frown. "Well, yes, but—"

"Then all is in order."

The steward grumbled but took the invitation. I leaned over the table as he wrote *William Kay, Scotland* onto the list with the other knights.

"The tournament begins this afternoon," the steward said, not meeting my eye. "All knights will receive their first-round opponents then. Official tournament lances will be provided, but every knight must have his own horse. A duel consists of a maximum of three passes. One point is awarded for a strike to the body or head, three points for breaking a lance, and unhorsing an opponent is an automatic victory. Any blow to a horse is cause for disqualification."

The steward finished reciting the rules and then glared at me.

"Thank you," I said. "I'll inform Sir Kay."

I turned to go, but Sir Payne stood in my path. "England

welcomes a Scot brave enough to enter the Tournament of Champions. Especially one who has such . . . taste in squires." He smiled and bowed his head. "I look forward to facing your lord on the track."

"Thank you, my lord. I'll tell him of your kindness."

I turned to go, but Sir Payne caught my arm. He gave me a wolfish grin. "And tell him, I collect my debts."

I yanked my hand free and hurried out of the tent. I untied Snowfoot and crossed to the far side of the tournament field where workers were constructing viewing stands. Beyond that, I found a modest stable away from the main road. The stable boy was thrilled to hear Snowfoot was in the tournament and lent me a stall for free, bringing fresh water for his trough. "A fine horse," the boy said. "Four socks will surely spell bad luck for his opponents."

I thanked the boy and closed the stall's gate behind me. I unpacked my travel sacks and hid what few possessions I had beneath the hay. I pulled out pieces of wrapped sausage and an apple I had stashed in my pack.

Things had moved fast since leaving Gowyn's farm. Now that my anger had subsided, I regretted how I'd left things. Gowyn had opened his home to me. He'd trained me and turned me into a knight in spirit. Though I wished he was there with me, I understood he had to keep his oath.

And I had an oath of my own to fulfill.

"We're here, boy," I said. "There's no turning back now."

Snowfoot snorted.

"I'm not worried either. I have you, after all." I took a deep breath and patted his head. "Come on. Time to get ready. We have a tournament to win."

The Tournament of Champions

Cheers and shouts filled the tournament grounds. I guided Snowfoot toward the noise, struggling to see through my closed visor. I breathed, trying to calm my nerves and not get sick—there was no removing my helmet now. Guards stopped me at the gates to the tournament field. I grunted and gave my father's name in my deepest voice. Sweat trickled down my brow as the guards looked from me to the tournament board.

"Where is your squire, Sir Kay?" a guard asked.

I cleared my throat; the sound echoed in my helmet. "I've no need of a squire."

Satisfied, the guards moved the gates and permitted me into the holding area. I sighed with relief. The charade had worked.

Now, I just had to survive the first round.

On the tournament field, three jousts were taking place at once. The armored knights looked like giants, charging at each other on monstrous beasts. On the first track, the knights collided in a violent explosion of shattered lances that sent one man flying off his horse. The crowd erupted.

I peered through the slit in my helmet to the royal pavilion above the first track. In the center of the nobles, in a high-backed seat, sat the King of England. The face below the crown was stern, as if surveying a battlefield. Perhaps he was.

The victorious knight rode before the royal pavilion. He leaned back, and his horse reared, kicking its hooves to mighty applause. The knight wore black armor. A wolf's head adorned the front of his helmet, and a flowing red-feathered plume trailed from the back.

"The winner," the tournament barker called in a booming voice. "Sir Edward Payne of England!"

The knight removed his helmet and waved to the crowd, his sweaty black hair matted to his forehead. My jaw tightened at the sight of the arrogant noble from the tournament tent. His opponent still lay in the dirt. Squires dragged the fallen knight from the field. My breath caught as I remembered my father's lifeless form. I knew that could easily be me. With no one, not even a squire to carry my body off the field.

My stomach tightened; my pulse raced. I took a breath, recognizing the fear streaming through my body. I was walking the high board again. I gave the fear a moment to sound its warning and then I exhaled, releasing the feeling in a slow breath. "It's jousting," I whispered to myself. "The field is bigger, nosier, but it's still jousting. That I can do."

With the closest of the three lists cleared, the barker announced the next duel.

"Sir Robert Dumont of England!"

The crowd cheered as a tall knight in shining armor rode from a separate holding area. He waved his lance proudly, trotting his horse in a circle.

"And his opponent," the barker called. "Sir William Kay of Scotland!"

It was like a spear rammed my insides. I'd waited my whole life to prove myself in a tournament, and now that the moment had come, I wanted to be anywhere else.

I quieted my mind and listened to the voice of my inner knight.

Bravery.

I rode Snowfoot onto the tournament field to a roar of boos. I was nothing like the other knights: I had no squire by my side, my father's armor was dented, my horse was smaller than the other knights' great warhorses and wore no coat or trappings. And worst of all, I was a Scot.

With no squire, I had to ride to the tournament rack and draw my own lance. The weapon felt heavy in my shaking hand. My head spun as I directed Snowfoot to the end of the track. It felt as if my armor had cracked open and the thousands of spectators could see the frightened girl inside. How did I think I could compete here? Surely I would be revealed as a fraud.

I notice I'm feeling like a fraud.

I looked up through the slit in my visor to the wall of clouds above. Somewhere behind all that grey was a blue sky. I just had to clear the clutter. I breathed and focused on my routine. I adjusted my helmet and tightened my grip on my lance. But the noise of the crowd was overwhelming.

The knight marshal walked to the center of the track, flag in hand. He looked at my opponent on the far end. Sir Dumont's armor glimmered in the grey afternoon light. The English knight raised his lance. The knight marshal turned to me.

"All right, Snowfoot," I said. "Let's do this."

I raised my lance. The red flag snapped into the air.

"Yah!" Snowfoot galloped down the right side of the rope barrier. The armor rattled around me. My vision came and went under the shifting visor. When the track bounced into view again, the English knight was upon me; his lance extended toward my heart. I flinched, dropping my lance and leaning away. My opponent's lance struck my hip as Snowfoot veered off the track.

The crowd erupted in boos and jeers. I stopped at the end of the track, catching my breath. My heart was racing. It had happened so fast.

"One point for Sir Dumont," the barker yelled. "If Sir Kay breaks off again, he will be disqualified."

Down the track, Sir Dumont was turning around and preparing for the second pass. I looked back to where my lance lay in the dirt. I didn't have a squire to fetch it for me. Cringing, I climbed down from Snowfoot and shuffled awkwardly in my armor toward the fallen lance.

Laughter filled the tournament grounds. I couldn't bend, so I had to kneel to the ground and swipe for my lance. My face burned as I picked up my lance and struggled back to Snowfoot. I climbed into the saddle and steadied myself, tuning out the jeers. "They won't stop me," I whispered, biting back the embarrassment. "I won't let them win."

I remembered Gowyn's lesson on mindfulness and didn't hide the feelings rushing through me. Instead, I named them: "There is embarrassment... There is anger."

Across the track, Sir Dumont raised his lance. The knight marshal motioned to me. I didn't raise my lance. Instead, I imagined a line in the dirt before me, separating the thinking ground from the trusting ground. I'd trained hard over the past months; I deserved to be here.

I pushed away the voice of fear and listened to my inner knight. *Resilience.*

Murmuring grew louder as everyone waited for my signal. I took a deep breath and focused on my opponent's glimmering armor. A new wave swept through my mind: "There is determination."

I set my focus on one thing: *Act bravely*. Then I inched Snowfoot across the line onto the trusting ground. I raised my lance. "Let's joust."

The red flag snapped, and I spurred Snowfoot down the track. The noise of the crowd faded. I aimed all my focus at my opponent. The bright, shining target.

Sir Dumont charged with frightening speed. The rope barrier separating us was so thin, we seemed sure to collide. Sir Dumont arched back, preparing to ram his lance through me. This time, I didn't flinch. I drove my lance forward into Dumont's exposed torso.

Before he could finish his powerful thrust, my lance struck his breastplate. The hit was square and true. Splinters pelted my helmet. Blind, I grabbed Snowfoot's neck. He screeched and carried me away from the collision.

When Snowfoot finally stopped, I sat up and saw my lance was broken. I looked back and down the track. Sir Dumont lay on the ground, trying to roll over, his armor sullied with dirt.

"The winner, Sir William Kay of Scotland!" the barker called. The crowd grumbled. Snowfoot snorted and raised his head.

"Sir Kay . . ." the barker said, waving to me expectantly. I thought of how Sir Payne had removed his helmet after victory, and I froze. I looked through the slit of my visor to the royal pavilion. The King of England waited with a grim look on his face.

I gulped and led Snowfoot forward. I tried to bow, but my armor didn't allow me. Unable to remove my helmet, I raised my visor in quick salute.

Murmurs spread through the royal pavilion. The king narrowed his eyes, studying me. Surely he saw I was an impostor. He would order his guards to seize me any moment.

Then came movement from the chair beside him. A girl in a bright blue gown stood up and applauded. "Well done, Sir Kay of Scotland. Well done."

The king shot the girl a severe look. Then, reluctantly, joined her in a half-hearted applause. The crowd followed suit.

I sighed and hurried off the field. It wasn't until I'd reached the safety of the holding area that the victory sank in. My gauntleted hands shook on Snowfoot's reins, and I beamed inside my helmet. I'd done it! I'd defeated a champion knight!

But the momentary elation was cut off by a violent crash as the duels resumed.

I'd survived the first round. But the tournament had only begun.

Reflection

My second duel took place late in the afternoon. My nerves had calmed considerably by then. I rode smooth and fast, striking out relentlessly at my German opponent. I broke two lances on his breastplate and scored a point on his visor in the last pass to win decisively. The English crowd wouldn't cheer for a Scot, but the gasps when I scored were praise enough.

Snowfoot held his head high as we walked from the tournament grounds, and I felt similar pride. I'd competed well at the Tournament of Champions and brought honor to my father's name. I could almost feel his eyes upon me. I hoped he was proud.

"We did good, boy," I said as Snowfoot chewed hay in the quiet stable. "I only wish Gowyn was here to see."

I knew then what I had to do. I hid my armor under a blanket and covered it with straw. Then I threw on my travel cloak and led Snowfoot out into the crowded streets of York. I feared someone would recognize Snowfoot with his white feet, but the people paid us no mind. To them, I was just a common girl. Hearty voices recounted favorite moments from the tournament. I smiled under my hood at the mention of "that tough Scot, Sir Kay."

When we reached the main road, Snowfoot broke into a gallop. I didn't need to direct him; he knew the way.

The sun had set by the time we reached Gowyn's farm. Even in the dim light, the rolling hills and the dirt track were a welcome sight. Shadow came to life as I rode up the path, huffing and racing circles around his corral. I reached the house and climbed down from Snowfoot.

"Stay here, boy," I said, but Snowfoot had a mind of his own. He wandered down the hill to the apple tree. I couldn't help but smile. Snowfoot was stubborn, but he was also the best horse a knight could ask for.

The door opened behind me. Gowyn filled the frame. I hesitated, suddenly worried I'd made a mistake in returning. Gowyn raised a bushy grey eyebrow. "Back to steal more apples?"

I shrugged. "They're finally ripe."

"Well, don't just stand there in the dark." Gowyn stepped back into the house, and I followed him inside. A pot warmed on the stove, and he offered me a plate. I should have declined, but my hunger outweighed my manners, and I soon polished off the plate, plus what was left in the pot.

"I'm glad to see you still in one piece," Gowyn said.

"I'm sorry for how I spoke to you, Gowyn. I had no right. After everything you've done for me . . ."

"I'm glad you came back, Meridian." From the way Gowyn looked at me, I knew all was forgiven. "Well, don't keep me waiting," he said. "Tell me about the tournament!"

"I'm still in it," I said, unable to hold back a smile. "I defeated two knights today."

"Congratulations."

"It's because of you, Gowyn. I couldn't have done it without your training."

"You hit the target. I merely straightened your aim."

It felt good to be in Gowyn's presence again. As hard as the months of training had been, I valued every moment. I knew the lessons I'd learned would shape me for the rest of my life.

"You've forged your own path. I'm proud of you, Meridian. And I'm sure your family would be proud, too."

I scoffed at the thought of my mother seeing me in armor, jousting against grown men. "I'm not sure you know my family."

"I know courage. The world is in short supply of it. No one could see what you're doing and not be inspired. That is a gift."

"Thank you, Gowyn. And as much as I want you to be there with me, I understand you must keep your oath. I know if your wife and daughter were here, they'd be proud of the man you've become."

Gowyn didn't move for a moment. Firelight flickered in his eyes. "Thank you, Meridian." He cleared his throat and shifted forward in his seat. "Now, are you ready to go over your duels?"

I looked up confused. "But I won."

"Don't let winning stop you from learning. There are always lessons, even in victory."

"Of course," I said, glad to have Gowyn at my side again.

"Let's start with what went well."

I went through my duels, describing every pass. Reflecting on my performance, I was naturally drawn to my mistakes and missed opportunities. But Gowyn reminded me to "hunt the good stuff."

"I didn't back down," I said. "Even after the embarrassment of dropping my lance."

"It could have been easy to let that embarrassment get to you. But you got back up and regained your focus. That showed resilience."

After discussing what went well, we went through areas of improvement and what I could do better the next day.

"I let the crowd get to me at times. All that booing made me angry. I felt rushed, wanting to get the pass over with and show them."

"What will you do when the crowd boos you tomorrow? What will you do if you feel rushed?"

"I'll stay in my three-foot world, focusing on what I can control. And I'll take more time in the thinking ground, not crossing to the trusting ground until I'm ready."

After evaluating the tournament, I felt more prepared and was eager to compete again. Gowyn stood and cleared the table. "We discussed the tournament," he said. "Now let it go."

"Let it go?"

"It's taxing to spend too much time analyzing the past or worrying over the future. You set aside time to reflect and learn, and now that time is over." He handed me the dirty bowls and cutlery. I took them to the basin and washed them out. I focused on the task, the feel of the water on my hands, trying to stay present. "When you're washing, wash," as my father would say.

When we'd finished cleaning, Gowyn walked me to the barn. When we reached the door he handed me the lantern. "Get some rest," he said. "You need to recover to perform your best. I'll have breakfast ready for you in the morning."

"Thank you, Gowyn. For everything."

Snowfoot was waiting for me in the barn. I unsaddled him and hugged him goodnight. I found my cot still there, the blankets neatly folded, and a fresh bucket of water on the floor. I smiled; Gowyn had expected me.

I lay on the bed and blew out the lantern's candle. Darkness covered me. I thought it would be impossible to get the tournament out of my head, but I faded fast, carried to sleep by the sound of Shadow's hoofbeats in the night.

The Wager

I woke the next day rejuvenated. I felt more prepared to compete after discussing the tournament and spending the night in an actual bed. But more than that, I'd patched things up with Gowyn. So it was in high spirits that I set off for York for the second day of the Tournament of Champions.

When I arrived, the tournament field was already filling with eager spectators. Peasants who couldn't afford a seat in the viewing stands stood around the outer fence. In the streets, people parted to make way for the carriages carrying the noble lords and ladies. I checked the tournament board for my first duel and then hurried to the stables where I'd left my armor. An hour later, Sir William Kay emerged ready to compete.

The second day of the tournament was more difficult than the first. Each round, the speed of the knight's horses grew faster, and the strength of their blows grew more powerful. I took hits that bruised through the armor and nearly knocked me to the ground. But I stayed in my saddle, undaunted. I couldn't ask for a more courageous ally than Snowfoot. As duels went on, the crowd stopped mocking the small, white-footed horse. Snowfoot charged fearlessly against the great warhorses, matching their fight.

I executed the plan Gowyn and I had discussed. Taking my time in the thinking ground to strategize and get the crowd's jeers out of my head. Each time fear felt too overwhelming, I embraced my inner knight and stepped onto the trusting ground with one clear focus. I faced opponent after opponent, treating them as gifts. Each knight posed a different challenge, a new puzzle to solve. I made adjustments without judgment, outscoring my opponents on the second pass and dominating the third. At the end of the second day of the tournament, I trotted off the field as one of only four remaining knights.

I reached the stable and climbed down from Snowfoot, holding a post for support. My armor felt twice as heavy. Pain radiated from every joint. But I was still standing.

"You were amazing today," I said, leading Snowfoot into the stall. "One more day like that and we'll ride away with the title and enough money to end my family's debts twice over."

The thought of family dampened my cheer. I'd been away from home and focused on my training for so long, I'd thought little of my mother and what she must be going through. I felt guilty for abandoning her, but she would never have allowed me to joust. And now that I'd tasted the thrill of competition, I didn't see how I could go back to the life of a lady. A life without victory.

Lost in my thoughts, I didn't hear the men enter the stable. I had begun to unstrap my armor when a voice called out, "Ah, the mysterious Sir Kay."

I pulled my helmet back on and spun around. Sir Edward Payne strode to the center of the stable, flanked by three men with sword belts. Payne no longer donned his black armor but a fine red tunic. He rested a hand on the hilt of his longsword as he looked around. "I see you've found a stable befitting a Scottish lord."

Snowfoot snorted and stomped. I hushed him and stepped out to meet Sir Payne, my heart racing.

"You jousted well today, Sir Kay," Payne said. "Curious. I've competed in every major tournament, and I've never heard of you." Sir Payne looked past me. "Where is your squire? A beautiful, spirited girl, if a little brawny."

"I sent her on an errand," I said in a deep voice.

Payne looked me over. "There's no need for armor. The dueling is done—for the moment."

I held my ground, keeping my visor closed. "What do you want?"

Sir Payne grinned, but there was nothing friendly in the expression. "The king may have signed a treaty with Scotland, but we both know peace will not last. My countrymen who died in battle will not be forgotten at the stroke of a pen."

Sir Payne leaned closer. I squinted, afraid he would recognize me through my eye-slit.

"Until then, this is our war," he said. "And it's a war I will not let you win."

Blood rushed through. Anger clouded all thoughts of danger, of the armed men at Payne's side. All I saw in Payne's face was a target I wanted to strike. "We'll see about that."

"You really think you have a chance? If you're so confident, would you care to wager? Say fifty pounds. Or are you filthy Scots all talk?"

"I'm happy to take your money," I growled.

"Then it's agreed. Sir William Kay wagers fifty pounds that he will win the Tournament of Champions. And we have witnesses to attest."

"Aye," Payne's companions confirmed.

Payne smirked at his own cleverness. "It will be nice owning land in the North. After I clear it of its barbaric people. Perhaps your lovely squire can deliver my earnings to me." He stepped back and gave a mock bow. "Good night, Sir Kay."

Payne sauntered out of the stable, followed by his men.

I turned and kicked the wooden post, cursing my foolishness. Once again, my temper had gotten me into trouble. Payne had goaded me to wager money I didn't have. And not just to defeat him, but the entire tournament field.

That night I rode to Gowyn's farm with my head down, my earlier excitement replaced with dread. Now I had more than the tournament to worry about. If I lost the wager to Sir Payne, I'd never get out of York alive.

Sir Kay

I couldn't bear to tell Gowyn about the wager. I was too ashamed that after all my training, I'd let my emotions get the better of me. I was distracted during our reflection and had to force down the meal. The tournament was no longer about winning a title. Because of me, my family's home and lands were in danger.

"You're quiet tonight," Gowyn said.

I sighed and put on a brave face. "I'm just nervous about the final day of competition." I ran my finger along the table, tracing the grains of wood along their twisting pathways.

"When you're nervous or unsure how to proceed, it's helpful to reflect on your values. They act as a light, guiding your decisions and actions. Can you be who you want to be, regardless of the situation or the obstacles before you?" Gowyn's eyes twinkled in the firelight. "Do you remember your core values?"

"Bravery, presence, and resilience," I said.

"And what would it look like to live out those values tomorrow?"

I imagined myself standing on the tournament field, facing

Payne with the weight of my family's future on my shoulders. Fear rose in my mind like a beating drum, but I pushed past it to the quiet voice of my inner knight.

"I'd stand up to my opponents," I said. "Instead of cowering, I'd march proudly before the king and all of York. I'd live in the moment and compete with everything I had, no matter the cost."

Gowyn nodded. "Competition tests us. It reveals our character. But our values extend beyond competition. What would it look like to live out those values in the rest of your life?"

I looked away, suddenly aware of my cowardice. I'd been so focused on jousting, I hadn't considered how I'd failed to live up to my standards off the field. At home, I'd always wanted to be somewhere else. I'd run from my father's death and still feared returning. How could it be easier to face lance-wielding knights than my own mother?

I imagined my values as a lantern shining the way forward, and my inner knight not only a competitor, but my ideal self. What kind of person did I want to be?

"I'd follow my own path," I said. "And I wouldn't stop fighting for what I believed in."

"That sounds like a champion to me." Gowyn held my gaze. "Remember, it's not titles that define us, Meridian. It's our character. And in that, you've proven yourself noble as any knight."

I smiled. "To hear you say that is as good as the real thing."

Gowyn rubbed his beard and shrugged. "Why not make it official?"

"What?"

Gowyn rose to his full height, his hulking figure filling the room. "Kneel before me, Meridian Kay."

I shook my head and then saw Gowyn was serious. I dropped to one knee on the kitchen floor. Gowyn grabbed a knife from the table and stood over me. "Do you Meridian Kay promise on your faith to uphold the virtues of a knight?"

"Gowyn, what are you doing? You can't—"

But there was no humor on Gowyn's face. I bowed my head, feeling the gravity of his words.

"I do."

"Do you vow to act with honor and chivalry, in word and deed, to defend the defenseless, and fight in service of your lord against all enemies, in good faith and without deceit?"

"I do," I said, my voice quivering.

"Then it is my honor to knight thee." He tapped each of my shoulders with the blade of the knife. "Arise, Sir Kay."

I couldn't move at first. My mind reeled, remembering countless times I'd imagined this moment as a child, pretending to be someone else. For one beautiful moment, I let myself believe it was true. Then I opened my eyes to the real world. Gowyn had the power to knight another man, but not a girl.

"Arise, Sir Kay," Gowyn repeated.

I stood, tears running down my face. I didn't wipe them away. "Thank you, Gowyn. For everything."

Gowyn gripped my shoulder. "The honor is mine."

I found Snowfoot by Shadow's corral. I stopped at the fence and watched the great black horse run in the night. The wild horse that was skittish of people in the day, now moved with grace and freedom. I could have watched him for hours.

"Come on, boy," I said, pressing my head to Snowfoot's. "It's time to get some sleep."

I lay in bed that night, thinking about the tournament. But I was no longer weighed down by fear. Though Gowyn wouldn't be on the tournament field, he would still be at my side, his lessons forever a part of me—in my thinking and in my actions. Tomorrow I faced overwhelming odds, but I wasn't alone.

I touched my shoulders, thinking of the gift Gowyn had given me. Though the ceremony had been but a gesture, I felt somehow changed. Whatever challenges came, I would face them with bravery, presence, and resilience. I would face them as a knight.

The Fall

In the stable stall, I suited up for the last day of the tournament. My heart raced, and my hands shook as I cinched my armor in place. A few days ago, I didn't know if I'd even get in the tournament; now I was two duels away from victory. I picked up my helmet and stared into its face. If only my father were here.

Snowfoot snorted and nudged my head. I pushed him away with a smile. I admired the horse for a moment, his dark red color, the white around his ankles. "People are fools for thinking you're unlucky. You're the finest horse I've ever met." Snowfoot raised his head. "And you know it, too."

I pulled my helmet on and a sigh reverberated inside the metal. It was time.

We rode from the stables to the tournament field. Shouts and cheers erupted ahead of me. The other semi-final duel was already taking place, and from the sound of the English crowd, Sir Payne was winning.

I entered the holding area and watched as Sir Payne charged down the track in his black armor. I searched for a weakness, but the English champion's form was flawless. As the jousters met, Sir Payne thrust his lance with such power, it shattered against his opponent's visor, whipping the knight's head back at an impossible angle. The knight flew from his horse and struck the ground in a clatter of armor. He lay motionless as the dust settled around him.

"The winner, Sir Payne of England!" the barker yelled above the cheering crowd. I took a deep breath. If I won my next duel, I would face Payne in the finals.

While the track was cleared, I closed my eyes and noted what thoughts and feelings washed against the bow of my attention. "There is nervousness . . . There is excitement . . . There is anticipation . . . There is presence." But my mindfulness was interrupted by an unusual sound. The crowd outside my holding area had started chanting. It took me a moment to register what they were saying.

"Sir—Kay! Sir—Kay! Sir—Kay!"

Surprised, I looked at the stands and saw a small but rowdy group of supporters whose chants rose above the hostile English crowd. My heart leapt at the sound of their voices. My countrymen were here.

One of the supporters pushed his way to the edge of the stands and leaned over the railing. The man's red face beamed as he shouted into the holding area. "Word throughout Scotland was one of our own was beating the pants off the English. We couldn't miss that!"

"God bless you, Sir Kay!" another man shouted behind him.

"Sir—Kay! Sir—Kay! Sir—Kay!"

I smiled at the sound of my father's name ringing through the tournament grounds. I gave the group of Scots a salute, and their cheering doubled.

"Our next jousters," the barker called, stepping onto the track. "Sir William Kay of Scotland!"

For the first time, the cheers outweighed the boos as I rode onto the tournament grounds.

"Sir—Kay! Sir—Kay! Sir—Kay!"

I looked from the peasant stands to the royal pavilion. The King of England sat in his high-backed chair, glaring at me. He hadn't expected a Scot to make it this far, or for a Scot's name to be cheered on English soil. He hadn't counted on me.

"And his opponent," the barker called. "Sir Bertrand Durfort of France!"

A great grey warhorse trotted out from the separate holding area. The knight riding him was enormous. A plume of purple feathers rose from the top of his helmet, which he removed and bowed to the king. The crowd roared in support of the French champion.

I rode to the end of the track and began my routine, tuning out the king, the crowd, and everything outside my three-foot world. It was just me and Snowfoot. And we were ready.

When the flag went up, Snowfoot charged. We rode along the right side of the rope barrier to meet our opponent. It was clear within three strides that Sir Durfort was faster than any rider I'd faced. He was upon me in a second. I rushed to aim and had hardly started my thrust when his lance struck me in the helmet. The world snapped to black. I spun around, grasping for the saddle, trying to stay seated. Snowfoot slowed, and I caught myself on his pommel, saving myself from defeat.

"One point, Sir Durfort!" the barker shouted.

But the blow had cost me more than a point. My head rang as Snowfoot trotted to the end of the track. I shifted my helmet into place, blinking away the blurred vision. I breathed, trying to clear my head before the next pass, but a storm of thoughts flooded my mind. Sir Durfort was too fast, too powerful. Another strike could kill me.

I shook my dazed head and clung onto Snowfoot. "There is

fear," I said, acknowledging the feeling sweeping through me like a shiver.

It's just a feeling. I reminded myself. *It doesn't control you. Use the information.*

"There is resilience," I said, conjuring the feeling.

I gazed down the track at my opponent. Sir Durfort sat atop his grey warhorse, waiting for me. I'd come this far. I wouldn't let fear stop me. Taking a deep breath, I concentrated on Sir Durfort's breastplate, setting my intention: "There is focus." I ushered Snowfoot onto the trusting ground. Then I raised my lance.

The red flag moved in the corner of my vision, but my eyes stayed on my target—not where it was, but where it was going to be. All thoughts left my mind, all fears, all cares. All I saw was Sir Durfort's breastplate, and my lance striking it.

It was a clean hit. My lance shattered on impact.

Sir Durfort's lance swept past my helmet. He'd taken another shot at my head. This time, missing by inches.

"Three points, Sir Kay!" the barker shouted.

The cheers from the Scots overwhelmed the crowd. They were on their feet, dancing in the stands.

I grabbed a new lance from the rack. Across the track, Sir Durfort rode toward the holding area, cursing. His squire ran out, carrying a lance. Sir Durfort kicked the lance out of his squire's hands and pointed back to the holding area. He was rattled. I led the French champion three points to one with one pass left. If I could just stay on my horse and avoid a direct shot, I'd advance to the finals. Excitement swept through me. The image of me standing atop the Tournament of Champions formed in my mind—

"No." I snuffed out the thought. *Stay present. What matters is the task at hand.*

Across the track, the squire carried another lance to Sir

Durfort. A red sash draped from its handle. The squire ran back to the holding area and stood beside a knight in black armor. What was Sir Payne doing there? The English champion stared at me across the tournament field, a smile on his face.

I turned away, trying to put Payne's face out of my mind. But I couldn't quell the anger burning inside. Suddenly, winning the round wasn't enough. I wanted to prove to Durfort, to Payne, to the King of England and everyone watching that I wasn't a pretender. I was as much a knight as any of them.

"Come on, Snowfoot," I said, raising my lance. "Let's knock a lord off his horse."

Snowfoot grunted and stomped his hoof. The knight marshal raised the flag, and we took off. Snowfoot rode with everything he had, matching Sir Durfort's warhorse stride for stride. Sir Durfort drew closer, and I focused on his breastplate. I drew my lance back and prepared to thrust with all my strength.

Then the French Knight did something unexpected. Instead of striking at my head, he thrust downward. It was as if Snowfoot slammed into a wall. For a moment, I was flying. Then I hit the ground with such force the world went black. When I opened my eyes, there were clouds. I was on my back, staring at the sky. The pain of realization struck me before the pain in my body. I'd been unhorsed. My back ached. Blood trickled down my cheek, and my tongue traced the space of a missing tooth. But it didn't matter. I'd lost.

An awful shriek rose above the noise of the stadium. Suddenly, none of my pain mattered.

"Snowfoot!"

I tilted my head, looking through the mud-filled slit in my visor. Snowfoot lay on his side, screaming, straining to get up. The lance was wedged in his chest.

"No." I groaned and rolled over in my heavy armor. Then I crawled across the dirt toward my horse. "No, no, no!"

I collapsed beside Snowfoot, looking at the lance embedded in him. Somehow it had not broken. Blood poured from the wound, down his red coat, and into the dirt. He shrieked again, kicking at the dirt, unable to stand.

"Snowfoot," I said, cradling his head. His dark eyes settled on me and he stopped fighting. His breath came out in ragged gasps.

Over the stunned murmur of the crowd came the barker's voice. "Illegal strike. Sir Durfort is disqualified. Sir William Kay wins."

I barely registered the victory. The tournament no longer mattered. All I cared about was Snowfoot.

"Snowfoot," I said, my voice breaking. "Snowfoot, get up. Please get up."

But Snowfoot's head lay still on the dirt. Hands grabbed me. I batted them away and fell back on Snowfoot, sobbing in my helmet. "No. He's my horse. I won't leave him. Snowfoot!"

Choosing the Path

The tournament was put on hold. Field hands dragged Snowfoot into a cart and pulled him back to the stable. There, the stable master removed the lance and hastily bandaged the wound. Snowfoot was too weak to even whimper.

"It's no use," the stable master said, wiping blood from his hands. "He should be put down."

"No," I said through my helmet. "I won't allow it."

"You're only prolonging his suffering."

"Leave us."

"Sir Kay, you must—"

"Leave us!"

The stable master walked out, closing the doors behind him. When he'd gone, I fell to my knees beside the cart and sobbed. I tried to remove my helmet, but it was dented; a piece of metal dug into my cheek. I pulled harder, groaning as the metal scraped up my cheek to my temple before coming free. Blood trickled down my cheek. I removed my gauntlets and touched Snowfoot, running my hand over his coarse hair.

"I know you're in pain, boy. But I won't let you go. I can't."

I could hear sounds from the tournament; the crowd was

growing restless. The stable door creaked open behind me. I thought it might be the knight marshal calling me to the field, or perhaps Sir Payne coming to gloat and collect his money. I glanced at my dented helmet but couldn't even muster the energy to hide.

"Go away," I said from the stall. "I'm finished."

"Meridian?"

I froze at the sound of my name, and the voice that had called it.

"Mother?" I gasped. It was such a shock to see her that all the fight that had been holding me together drained from my body. I slumped to the ground.

Two others entered the stable behind my mother. My heart leaped at the sight of my cousin Roland and my handmaid, Eby. Roland hurried past my mother and fell beside Snowfoot. He lifted the horse's bandage and examined the wound. "I saw what happened." He shook his head. "A tournament lance couldn't have done this."

"What are you doing here?" I stammered. "How . . . how did you find me?"

"Imagine my surprise," my mother said, "to hear that my dead husband was competing in England." She looked at my bloody face. "Hasn't this sport taken enough from us?"

I shook my head. "You didn't understand father, and you don't understand me."

"I may not have understood your father, but I still loved him." My mother's hard exterior cracked for a moment as her eyes fell on my father's dented helmet. "I only wanted to protect you, Meridian. If I'd known it would push you away . . ." She straightened herself, pulling the hem of her dress off the dirty stable floor. "I've come to take you home."

I winced, remembering my wager with Payne. There wouldn't be a home to return to. "Mother, the money—"

"I've already seen to our debts. You will marry Jonathan Alison upon our return."

"Mother, you don't understand."

"You will do as you're told, Meridian! It's too dangerous for you here. If anyone discovers who you really are, you'll be arrested—or executed!" Her eyes could have melted the armor from my body. "I know marriage is not what you want right now, but it's the best I could do to ensure the future of our family."

I looked from my mother to Snowfoot, and I knew I had no choice. My time jousting was over.

"Eby, help my daughter get cleaned up and presentable," my mother said. "We will ride straight to Lord Alison's castle and complete this marriage before word of this . . . disgrace . . . gets out. I'll see about selling that armor before we leave the city. It's time this family was rid of jousting once and for all."

My mother looked down at me, her face pained.

"You'll thank me someday, Meridian. It's time to grow up and accept who you really are."

My mother turned and strode out of the stable, holding her dress. I was left speechless. After all my work, my mother had ridden to England and determined the course of my life.

"It is good to see you, my lady," Eby said, kneeling by my side. "It has been far too quiet without you."

"It's over," I said. "I'm to marry a man I've never met."

"He must be decent enough, or your mother never would have agreed. She cares about you, Meridian, though she doesn't know how to show it."

Eby ran a hand through my sweaty hair, her touch warm on my forehead. She frowned at my black eye and missing tooth. "What a bride you'll make. You're practically one giant bruise. I'll fetch some water and we'll get you cleaned off and feeling better in no time. Come, Roland."

Roland, who had been examining Snowfoot's wound, stood and dusted off his pants. "He'll need some tending and careful watch. But he's a tough horse. I'll make sure he pulls through."

I nodded, fighting back tears. "Thank you, Roland."

"I couldn't believe it was you out there," Roland said. "I wish Uncle William could have seen you joust. It was truly something special."

"Go on, Roland," Eby called. Roland nodded and hurried off. Eby gave me a tender smile. "Have courage, dear. You're strong enough to face whatever lays ahead."

Eby closed the stable door behind her, leaving me alone with Snowfoot. A trumpet sounded from the tournament field. The finals would wait no longer. Payne would be crowned champion without lifting a lance.

"I don't know if we could have beat him, boy," I said. "But I would have loved to try."

Snowfoot snorted weakly, never lifting his head. My father's helmet sat in the dirt beside him, the eye-slit staring at me. I picked it off the ground and felt its weight in my hands. Would Payne accept this dented armor as payment? I gritted my teeth at the thought of Payne or anyone else with my father's armor. It belonged to House Kay. It belonged to me.

Chants rose from the tournament field. They were calling for Sir Kay.

My father's name.

My name.

I took a deep breath and exhaled: "There is fear." But it wasn't the fear of losing. It wasn't the fear of imprisonment or dying. It was the fear of walking away. Then, through the fear, came the voice of my inner knight. *Bravery. Presence. Resilience.* I remembered the oath I'd made. I had no horse, my armor was in shambles, and I could barely stand. But I wouldn't stay down.

I lifted my helmet and forced it back over my head. I grimaced as the dented metal cut a fresh path down the side of my face. In this armor, the world saw a knight. So that's who I'd be.

I climbed to my feet and staggered out of the stable, back toward the tournament field. I didn't know what awaited me at the end of this path, but I would face it on my feet.

When I reached the tournament grounds, the place was in an uproar. Spectators in the viewing stands, feeling robbed of a final, grew unruly. The knight's marshal and the tournament barker huddled below the royal pavilion. On a table before them sat the prize—a golden horse. Sir Payne stood to the side, helmet removed, ready to accept the prize and the tournament title.

A guard held out a hand, barring my path. Then, recognizing my armor, he opened the gate and let me pass. A cheer rose from the Scottish corner as I entered. But their shouts faded at the sight of me. My body ached, my cheek burned, but I walked on. The chaos in the stands hushed as I limped across the tournament field.

Sir Payne's face twisted into a sneer. "I didn't think you were going to show," he said. "Or have you just come to bring me my winnings?"

It took all my effort not to knock the grin off Payne's face. I pushed past him and stood before the royal pavilion. The king glared at me from his high-backed chair. Beside him, his daughter touched a hand to her chest.

"Sir Kay," the knight's marshal said. "We were about to withdraw you from the final. Can you continue?"

"I'm here," I said. "But I have no horse."

"If you cannot mount, Sir Payne will be awarded the title by forfeit."

"I do not forfeit."

The nobles' murmurs spread like a wave through the crowd.

"Perhaps the Scot means to joust on foot," Payne said.

"I've earned my place in the finals," I said. "Give me a horse and I'll joust."

"The rules are clear. Every knight must provide his own horse. This is the Tournament of Champions, not a charity."

I spun toward Payne. "Are you afraid to face me?"

"You dare insult me!" Payne snapped. The black-armored knight strode forward until he stood over me. "Who do you think you are?"

I squinted through the slit in my visor—at Payne, at the King of England, at the thousands of people surrounding me. After everything I'd been through, my path led me here.

My mother was right: it was time to accept who I really was.

Bravery.

I removed my helmet. A cool wind blew my hair free as I stared defiantly at Payne.

"I am Meridian Kay," I said. "And I am a knight!"

Meridian Kay

The King of England pounded his armrest. "What is the meaning of this?"

All eyes fell on me. The entire stadium seemed to draw in a collective gasp. It was silent. I dropped to a knee and bowed my head, if only to give myself time to recover my voice. "My name is Meridian Kay, Your Majesty. Daughter of Sir William Kay."

"Where is your father?" The king looked around the tournament field, confused. "Are his injuries so great that he would send his daughter?"

"My father died months ago, Your Majesty. I am here, competing in his place."

The king scowled. "This is no time for jest, girl."

"It's the truth. I've defeated every champion thus far. And I have the bruises to prove it."

A new quake of gasps rippled through the crowd, reaching even the peasants on the outer fence. No one could believe the brave Scot who'd defeated knight after knight for the past three days was really a girl.

"Impossible," Payne yelled. "You make a mockery of His Majesty's tournament."

"If this is true, then Sir Payne wins by forfeit," the knight marshal said. "The lady is not eligible to compete. For she is not a knight."

The word of "forfeit" circled through the crowd. Boos and outrage filled the air. The people had waited days for this moment. They wanted a duel.

The king stood, his face red. "By posing as a knight, you have violated not only the sanctity of the tournament, but English law."

Movement in the crowd caught my attention. My mother pushed her way to the front of the stands. She stared at me, eyes wide with terror.

The guards circled me, hands on their swords, ready to deal punishment at the king's command. I wanted to run, to disappear into the crowd, but there was no escape. I kept my head held high. Then the king's daughter rose and spoke in his ear. The king frowned. "Hold," he called, stopping the guards. He settled back into his seat. "Seeing as the purpose of this tournament is to celebrate peace between our nations, I am willing to grant mercy. Admit your lie, and your life will be spared."

"My lie, Your Majesty?"

"Clearly you are not the one who defeated the field of champions. You are only a girl."

My mind spun. I'd been offered a way out. Flee and I might live. But a voice spoke through me, charging ahead. "I do not lie." I rose to my feet and stood before the king. "I earned my place in the finals, and if I had a horse, I would finish the tournament."

"Meridian, no!" my mother screamed.

The king smirked. "So be it," he said. "For the crime of falsely impersonating a knight, I have no choice but to sentence you to—"

"Wait!" a voice boomed across the tournament field. All

heads turned to the man who would dare interrupt the king. A hulking figure in brown farmer's clothes strode across the field as calmly as if he were the victor come to accept his prize. The grey-haired man pushed through the guards to stand at my side.

"Gowyn," I gasped. "What are you doing here?"

"I came to see how you were doing." He looked at the circle of armed guards and nodded. "About what I expected."

A wave of gratitude rushed through me. Gowyn had come.

"Enough," Payne called. "Who is this man who interrupts the king? And how did he get on the field?"

"My name is Gowyn Stowe of Hill End."

"Sir Gowyn the Grey?" Payne looked skeptically at the old man standing before him. The name "Grey Knight" passed through the crowd as people craned their heads to see the legendary champion.

"It doesn't matter," Payne stammered. "The king has made his decision."

"Sir Gowyn, is that really you?" The king leaned forward in his chair.

Gowyn stepped before the royal pavilion and dropped to a knee. "Yes, Your Majesty."

"It's been so long," the king said, his voice softening, as if speaking to an old friend. "I'd thought you'd died."

"Not yet, Your Majesty."

"What are you doing here?"

Gowyn slowly rose to his feet and stood before the king. He spoke in a commanding voice that could be heard across the tournament field. "The war cost each of us. After so much fighting, so much loss, I couldn't go on. I told myself I was mourning, but really I was hiding from the world. Then Your Majesty's tournament drew me out. I was inspired by the bravery seen here, by someone who exemplifies the traits of a courageous and honorable knight. You created this tourney to celebrate the end of our war with Scotland. Therefore, as a symbol of peace, it would be my honor to offer myself as squire to Sir Kay."

I gasped, touching a gauntleted hand to my breastplate. Murmurs of shock spread through the crowd. The Grey Knight offering to squire for a Scot?

"Don't be preposterous," the king said. "She's but a girl making false claims. She is no knight."

"I'm afraid that isn't true, Your Majesty." Gowyn glanced back at me with a sly grin. "For I knighted her myself."

Shouts filled the stadium. The crowd could no longer hold its astonishment. Calls of outrage were outweighed by cheers. Then, from the section of my countrymen, came a yell above all the others: "Let them joust!" A roaring applause followed. Regardless of the riders, the people wanted a final duel.

The king was calling for silence, but the crowd was too loud. Then the king's own daughter jumped to her feet and joined the applause. The passion of the people was so great, the king had no choice but to surrender.

"Very well," he said, waving a hand. "The finals shall commence. Take the field, *Sir* Kay."

The stadium erupted.

Gowyn bowed to the king and stepped toward me. "Looks like we're in this together now."

"I can't believe you did that," I said. "I can't believe you're here. What about your oath?"

"I swore an oath never to leave my family," Gowyn said. "That's why I'm here."

I threw myself at him. The embrace was clumsy in my armor, but I squeezed him just the same. "Thank you," I said. "But I can't joust. I don't have a horse."

Gowyn smiled. "Did you think I walked here?"

He waved to the holding area. There followed a commotion as the stable boy struggled with the reins of a great black horse.

"Shadow?" I gasped. "He can't ride with all these people around. He'll throw me for sure."

"You'll just have to lead him."

"It seems Sir Kay has found a horse," the tournament barker called. "Let the final round of His Majesty's Tournament of Champions begin!"

The crowd roared. Gowyn took Shadow's reins. The stable boy fled, happy to be rid of the crazy horse.

"Sir Kay," Gowyn said, offering his hand.

Shadow cried and pulled against the reins, a wild animal fighting to be free. I took Gowyn's hand. He helped me into the saddle as the horse bucked beneath me.

"I don't know if this is a good idea," I said.

Gowyn handed me the reins. "You'll just have to trust each other."

Shadow jostled and stomped his feet. The noise of the crowd was terrifying him. I thought he might explode down the track and off the tournament field.

"Easy, boy," I said, "Calm down."

"Sir Kay," a voice called from the royal pavilion. The king's daughter leaned over the railing and held out a long white scarf. "A token for your bravery."

I wrangled Shadow forward. The horse kicked and tried to throw me, but I clung on.

"Thank you, Your Highness," I said, taking the scarf.

"Best of luck," she said. Then, lowering her voice to a whisper, "Show them what you can do."

I nodded and slid the scarf down into the wrist of my gauntlet. When I turned Shadow around, Payne was waiting for me. He glared at me from atop his horse. "You may have fooled the others. But I'll make sure you don't leave this field in one piece." He kicked his horse and stormed down the track.

Gowyn approached, carrying my dented helmet. "This has seen better days."

"I see better without it, anyway."

"Watch his lance. He'll want to save face by finishing this in one pass. Your exposed head makes an appealing target."

There was movement near the trophy table. The knight marshal was speaking to the tournament barker. The tournament barker looked at the king for confirmation. Then he walked to the center of the track and faced the crowd of spectators.

"For the final joust," the barker shouted. "The tilt barrier will be removed!"

Men ran to the track. They removed the poles and dragged away the rope that separated the two sides of the track. Not only would I be competing against Payne without a helmet, on a horse I couldn't control, there would be no barrier separating us.

I turned and found my mother in the crowd. She shook her head, pleading with me not to go through with it. I thought of obeying, of climbing down from Shadow and running to her, to home, to safety. But a voice cut through those thoughts. *What kind of person do you want to be?*

"This is what you've trained your whole life for," Gowyn said, holding up a lance. "Trust yourself."

Bravery. Presence. Resilience.

Embracing my inner knight, I took the lance.

It was time to joust.

The Finals

Shadow screeched and swung his head, trying to get away from the cheering spectators. "Easy, Shadow," I said. "Easy." But Shadow's panic spread through me. I stood before thousands of people with no helmet to hide behind. Frightened thoughts filled my mind. *There's no way I can win. The world is going to see I'm a fake. I'm not good enough!*

Then I took a breath and detached the thought.

I'm having the thought, I'm not good enough.

A breath.

I notice I'm having the thought, I'm not good enough.

Another breath. I exhaled, releasing the thought. It had no control over me.

I yanked on the reins and wrestled Shadow into position. "Come on, Shadow. We can do this."

Payne waited for me on the other end of the track. His black armor and wolf's-head helmet were designed to strike fear, and I felt plenty of it. If I lost this duel, he would claim my family's land.

The crowd hushed as the knight marshal carried the flag to

the center of the open track. He looked to his right. Payne raised his lance. The knight marshal turned to me.

Steady. Don't signal until you're committed.

I took a breath and focused on one thing: *Attack the target.* I crossed onto the trusting ground and raised my lance.

The flag shot into the air.

"Yah!" I cried. Shadow burst forward with so much speed I toppled back, squeezing my legs and trying to stay in the saddle. I pulled myself forward on the bouncing horse. Without my helmet, I had a clear view of Payne coming. The large black shape barreled toward me like a battering ram. There was no rope barrier separating us. We were going to collide.

I gritted my teeth and aimed my lance, pushing through my fear. Whatever happened, I wouldn't back down.

Then, just before collision, Shadow startled and swerved. Payne's lance glanced my side.

Point Payne. I never even attempted a strike.

I wrestled the frantic horse to a stop at the end of the track. "Steady," I said. "Steady!" But it was no use. All the speed in the world didn't matter if I couldn't control it. I replayed the first pass in my head, searching for a weakness in Payne's form. He was as disciplined as he was fierce. He rode coiled and tight until the moment he struck.

Down the track, Payne's lance was already raised. The knight marshal waited for my signal. The duel was moving too fast. I had no time to plan. It was taking all my effort just to stay on Shadow.

"Come on, Shadow," I pleaded. "Trust me."

The horse's heavy breathing settled. I raised my lance.

The second pass began in another blaze of speed. This time, I was ready for it. I leaned forward, aiming Shadow down the track five feet to the right of Payne. If I could keep Shadow steady, I'd have a chance.

Payne charged at me. I focused on his hunched body and drew my lance back. But at the last moment, Shadow balked again. My lance missed, and I teetered off-balance. I was exposed; my unprotected head lay vulnerable. I closed my eyes, bracing for a blow that would take my life. Payne's lance struck just below my throat, shattering against the top of my breastplate. My momentum stopped as wood shards pelted my face, and I flew out of my saddle.

I kept my eyes closed as I braced for impact with the ground. But the ground never came. I opened my eyes. The dirt track moved below me; Shadow's hooves thundering beside my ear. I reached out and felt the reins tangled around my leg. It was the only thing keeping me horsed.

I groaned and pulled myself up. The tournament field spun around me. I felt the dent in the top of my breastplate from Payne's blow. An inch higher, and I'd be dead.

Gowyn reached me, carrying my lance. "Are you all right?"

I fought back tears at the sight of him. "It's over."

"It's not over. You still have one more pass."

"I'm down four points. I can't score on him, let alone beat him. There's no reason to continue."

Gowyn grabbed Shadow's reins. "You continue because it's who you are. You're a knight, Meridian." He handed me the lance and backed away. "This is your moment. This moment, right now. Be here for it."

I stayed there with the lance across my lap, overwhelmed by the noise of the arena. Everyone had gathered for the final duel: the peasants along the outer fence, the nobles in their padded seats, my mother, Roland, and Eby standing with my cheering countrymen. So many people I didn't want to let down. The pressure was crushing. In the middle of the field, surrounded by thousands of people, I felt more alone than ever.

I tried my routine, noting the feeling aloud: "There is pressure." I took a deep breath and soaked in the feeling. Most people never get to feel this pressure, never get the opportunity to be in this big of a moment. I reached my arms out to the sides and then stretched them in front of me, tracing my three-foot world. The score, the title, my family's debts, the future—all these things were outside of my control. I couldn't determine how I finished. But I could determine how I fought.

"Ready, Sir Kay," the knight marshal called. The noise of the tournament field came back into focus, louder than ever. I grabbed the reins and led Shadow across the line to meet Payne. I started to raise my lance when I felt a flood of doubt. *You're not ready.* I stopped and pulled Shadow back across the line onto the thinking ground.

"Sir Kay," the knight marshal called impatiently. The packed stands stirred, restless of the delay.

My heart raced. I felt my presence slipping. I wanted to be anywhere but on the tournament field. Then I heard my father's voice, spoken from within me. *Remember to keep your head and your feet in the same place. When you're jousting, joust.*

I bit back tears. Remember my father—the man who, despite the law, had taught his daughter to joust—a new feeling rose inside me, overtaking all others: "There is gratitude."

I looked up at the cloudy sky. A crack in the grey revealed a sliver of bright blue beyond. A blue sky that was always there. I took a deep breath and exhaled, as if to blow the clouds away.

"Sir Kay!" the knight marshal called again. But I ignored him. I reached into the gap in my gauntlet and withdrew the long white scarf.

"There's no one here but us, Shadow." I placed the fabric over the horse's eyes and tied a knot, turning day to night. Then I whispered into his ear, noting the feeling welling inside me as a final command: "There is trust."

I raised my lance and led Shadow across the line onto the

trusting ground, the two of us now moving as one. As the flag rose for the final pass, only one thought remained in my mind: *Ride free!*

Shadow launched forward, and the world slowed around me. I was fully present, aware of everything: the sound of Shadow's hooves hitting dirt; the shift of weight as his muscles propelled us forward; the cool wind whipping against my face, blowing back my hair; my lance locking into place at my side, a part of me.

I rode straight at Payne.

Payne's shoulder slumped, blocking his breastplate, leaving no opening. He was an expert jouster with technique perfected from years of training. But I was a problem solver. I opened my eyes wide, taking in everything. Then, as if on its own, my hand pulled the reins, guiding Shadow to the left. Payne shifted, confused. Jousters always passed on the right. That's how it was done. But with no rope barrier, a new path emerged, and I took it, approaching Payne on the opposite side. I released the reins and gripped the lance with two hands. I trusted the instinct and threw all my weight behind the attack, abandoning defense to deliver the strike.

The tip of my lance struck Payne's visor. I kept thrusting, driving the lance through him. The lance exploded into splinters. Payne's head flew back. Then the rest of his body followed.

I dropped the broken lance and pulled Shadow to a stop. It wasn't until I turned around that I realized what I'd done. The English champion lay on the ground, black armor covered in dirt.

I'd unhorsed Sir Edward Payne. I'd won.

Instead of a roar of applause, the tournament field was silent. The crowd was stunned. I climbed down from Shadow and approached the royal pavilion. The king didn't move, his face contorted in anger. I stood before him, not cowering, not bowing. Before the king could speak, his daughter rose and clapped. The sound was soft, the flutter of a bird's wings, but it carried through the tournament field, growing louder as more and more people joined. Cheers erupted from the Scottish section with chants of "Sir—Kay! Sir—Kay! Sir—Kay!"

And then it was an uproar.

The king barked orders, but his words were lost in the noise of celebration. He pounded his armrest to be heard, but the crowd would not relent. The chants swept through the peasant section as they pushed against the fence, shouting "Sir—Kay! Sir—Kay! Sir—Kay!" Finally, the king fell back in his chair in surrender and waved a hand. The knight marshal carried the tournament trophy from the table.

"Well fought, Sir Kay," he said, handing me the golden horse.

A squire rushed onto the field to help Sir Payne to his feet. The English knight swatted him away and tore off his helmet.

"Oh, Sir Payne," I called.

Payne stopped and glared at me.

"I believe you owe me a debt," I said. "And I expect you to present it in person." I smiled and felt the pain of a black eye and a missing tooth. Payne sneered and stormed off the tournament field.

In the commotion, I saw my mother pushing through the crowd onto the track. She stopped before me. From the look on her face, I must have been a sore sight. "I . . . I can't believe what you did."

"Mother, with the prize purse, and a healthy donation from Sir Payne, we'll have more than enough to pay off our debts and keep our lands."

My mother studied me, the sternness gone from her face. "I don't want to argue, Meridian. All I ever wanted was a safe future for you."

"I know, Mother. But I'd rather have a happy one."

My mother sighed. "I suppose it won't be the first marriage that's been called off."

"Do you mean it?"

"Not that we'd have any choice once Lord Alison hears of this." She raised an eyebrow. "Or sees the state of his bride."

I stepped forward and wrapped my arms around her. "Thank you, Mother."

My mother returned the embrace, pressing against my armor. Then she pushed away, blinking away tears. "You are coming home then?"

I nodded. "Yes."

"Good," my mother straightened herself. "Then I will see about transportation."

"This might help," I said, handing her the golden horse.

"Certainly not," she said, holding it close. "This will go in a place of honor." She marched off the track, cradling the trophy, the hem of her dress dragging in the dirt.

I turned and looked through the crowded tournament field. A large black shape moved toward the exit. Gowyn was leading Shadow away.

"Gowyn," I called. "Gowyn, wait!" I raced through the crowd and caught him before the holding area. "You're leaving?"

"I realize now why I retired from tournaments in the first place," he said, struggling to hold Shadow. "They're too stressful."

"What you did for me, I'll never be able to repay."

"You did something special here, Sir Meridian Kay. Never forget that. I know I won't."

"Will I ever see you again?"

"I'm sure our paths will cross."

I smiled. "If you ever travel up north, I owe you some warm meals."

Gowyn ran a hand through Shadow's mane. "I might just do that." He bowed. "Sir Kay."

Emotions swept through me as Gowyn led Shadow through a mob of spectators. I knew I'd never forget what I'd learned and all he'd done for me. I took a deep breath, mindful of the moment.

"There is love," I whispered under my breath as Gowyn vanished into the busy streets of York.

Homeward

We rode home the following day on horses and a carriage bought courtesy of Sir Payne. Upon reaching the main road, I turned and watched York fade behind me, its twin spires raised defiantly above the city, like dueling lances.

I shifted in my saddle, not ready to leave it all behind just yet, as if distance and time would erase all I'd done. I didn't want to forget a moment of it, not even the pain. The soreness of my muscles, the bruises on my skin, were all reminders of what I'd accomplished. I took a deep breath and savored the moment and the feeling of pride I knew would pass.

The moment was broken by the sound of Roland's voice from the front of the carriage. "Did you see how she unhorsed him? Her lance went straight into his visor. Wham! I used to practice with her, you know. When is the next tournament, Eby? I want to sign up."

"Patience, Roland," Eby said. "I'm sure you'll find plenty of opportunities to bash your head in, too."

"Meridian." My mother's head emerged from the carriage window. I trotted the mare over to her. It felt strange to be with my family again. Away from Gowyn's farm and the single focus of jousting.

"I just wanted to say . . ." She looked down as if the words lay on the slowly passing ground. "I know you've been through a lot these past months. I see how it's changed you. You've had to grow up so fast since your father died, and I . . . I want us to . . ." She smiled, flustered. "I'm just glad you're coming home."

"Me, too," I said.

"And just because we called off the wedding with Lord Alison doesn't mean you don't plan on ever getting married, does it?"

I shrugged. "We'll see."

My mother rolled her eyes. "Bless my heart, I should have had a son."

I slowed the mare, letting the carriage pass. The attached cart bounced along the road. Snowfoot lay on his side atop some hay, his white feet dangling off the edge.

"Don't get used to loafing," I said. "We have a lot of work to do once you're healthy. I hear there's a big tournament in Paris next spring. We have a title to defend."

Snowfoot snorted. It was a welcome sound.

The sun was warm, the sky a clear blue. It was a beautiful day to be riding. We passed a field on the outskirts of York where two children played. They carried long sticks in their hands and charged at each other through the high grass. They yelled and thrust the sticks as they passed.

As we passed, the two children stopped and lowered their lances. From close up, I realized they were both girls. Their eyes went wide when they saw me. They whispered to each other and then waved excitedly.

I nodded and tipped an imaginary visor in salute.

Acknowledgments

Thank you to John Mayer for pushing me to write this book (even though he was skeptical about setting it in the world of jousting).

There are many coaches whose work have shaped the lessons in this book. Thank you to Bernie Holliday, who introduced me to the training and trusting mindsets and think box, play box. Peter Haberl, who introduced me to mindfulness and the importance of identifying your values. Ceci Craft, who introduced me to the concept of the three-foot world.

Thank you to my editors, Christie Hanzlik and Darsi Dreyer. To my wife, Janelle, who always sees my work at the roughest stage and encourages me to keep writing anyway. Early readers: John Mayer, Bernie Holliday, Peter Haberl, Kyle Cossairt, Paola Rodriguez, Deb Shepherd, Doug English, and Tom Black.

I'd like to thank all my coaches and teachers who helped shape me into the person I am today.

I hope this story inspires others to embrace their inner knights and to bravely pursue their own paths.

About the Author

Billy Ketch Allen grew up in Fallbrook, California, and studied creative writing at Cal State Northridge. He plays professional beach volleyball during the day and writes books at night.

www.billyketchallen.com

Made in the USA
Monee, IL
17 March 2022